CAPTIV

Brice claimed he would never trust Macy again. What chance, then, did their marriage have?

Books you will enjoy
by MARGARET PARGETER

THE ODDS AGAINST

After Petula Hogan had walked out on him, Carl Elliot had become a changed man, bitter and suspicious of all women. So had Gail done the right thing in agreeing to marry him? She had no doubt about her feelings for Carl—but would that be enough to make such a one-sided marriage work?

BORN OF THE WIND

While Sherry could see that a marriage between her brother and Scott Brady's sister might well be a disaster, as Scott had foretold, she really didn't see what she could do about it. And, anyway, what right had Scott to be so angry with *her*?

TOTAL SURRENDER

Neale Curtis had taken an instant dislike to her boss, Lawton Baillie. Until she was forced to join him on his yacht, when her feelings began to change—but that was dangerous, because he had made it perfectly clear what *he* wanted, and it wasn't what she wanted...

CAPTIVE OF FATE

BY

MARGARET PARGETER

MILLS & BOON LIMITED
15–16 BROOK'S MEWS
LONDON W1A 1DR

All the characters in this book have no existence outside the imagination of the Author, and have no relation whatsoever to anyone bearing the same name or names. They are not even distantly inspired by any individual known or unknown to the Author, and all the incidents are pure invention.

The text of this publication or any part thereof may not be reproduced or transmitted in any form or by any means, electronic or mechanical, including photocopying, recording, storage in an information retrieval system, or otherwise, without the written permission of the publisher.

This book is sold subject to the condition that it shall not, by way of trade or otherwise, be lent, resold, hired out or otherwise circulated without the prior consent of the publisher in any form of binding or cover other than that in which it is published and without a similar condition including this condition being imposed on the subsequent purchaser.

*First published in Great Britain 1985
by Mills & Boon Limited*

© Margaret Pargeter 1985

*Australian copyright 1985
Philippine copyright 1985
This edition 1985*

ISBN 0 263 75011 6

*Set in Monophoto Times 10 on 10½ pt.
01-0485 – 59171*

*Made and printed in Great Britain by
Richard Clay (The Chaucer Press) Ltd,
Bungay Suffolk*

CHAPTER ONE

MACY was in a hurry and driving too fast but she could have sworn the factory entrance was clear of all traffic as she took the corner leading to the car-park on practically two wheels. Where the powerful black car came from, she had no idea, but it was suddenly there, blocking the road and she was crashing into it. Not until her car door was wrenched open did she realise that it was the compound wall she had hit and not the vehicle belonging to the furious looking man who stood fuming down on her.

'Of all the brainless things to do!' he exploded, searing her with the anger in both his voice and eyes. His tirade against careless driving continued but Macy scarcely heard. There was a ringing in her ears and she felt suddenly sick.

'Please!' she whispered frantically, a hand flying to her mouth, 'I think I'm going to be . . .'

In a trice she was whipped around and her head pushed down. 'Use the road,' the man invited roughly, 'you've made a big enough mess of your car.'

Fortunately the sickness passed before she was forced to suffer further indignity but, on hearing his remark about her car, the feeling didn't leave her completely. She tried to focus dazed eyes on the wall against which her small runabout appeared to be crushed and a visible shudder shook her.

Horrified she turned back to the man who, despite his unrelenting anger, still supported her firmly. His face swam above her, she could just make out harsh dark features. 'Do you think there's much damage?' she gasped.

'To the wall or your car?'

She swallowed, wishing his voice had been kinder. 'Well, both.'

He didn't spare her. 'Your car will certainly need attention and the wall might have a crack in it.' Then his voice surprisingly softened as his eyes narrowed and he seemed to be seeing her white, shocked face for the first time. 'I shouldn't worry about the wall, if I were you. It might be in better shape than you are. How are you feeling?'

'I—I'm not sure,' she breathed as their eyes met. As she became lost in his intent grey gaze, Macy's heart lurched then threatened to stop beating altogether. The trembling in her slender body increased as she found she couldn't break the contact. It was incredible, after the shock she had just received, that something about this stranger's dark face should be attracting her like a magnet. She felt the whole of her being mesmerised by him to the extent that she was unable to look away.

It startled her further that he appeared to be as drawn to her as she was to him. She was conscious of his suddenly glittering eyes piercing her, as if trying to take in the whole of her in a few brief seconds.

Was he merely anxious over her condition? Hazily she decided this must be the reason for the intensity of his expression. She would have liked to have told him that the shaken state she was in might be as much a culmination of what had gone before, rather than what had just happened, but knowing the futility of trying to explain the unexplainable, she could only stare at him helplessly.

Summoning the last shreds of her willpower, Macy tore her eyes from his, wondering at the tightness of her chest. 'I'm sure there's nothing really wrong,' she murmured, 'I think I just got a fright.'

Letting go of her, the man shook his head, as though trying to rid himself of inexplicable feelings, yet there was an odd urgency in his voice when he spoke. 'If you're sure you are only shaken, there's a hotel I noticed, about a mile back along the road. You should have a rest and a drink.'

'I don't think I could walk that far,' she whispered, believing he was directing her.

'I'm not suggesting you walk,' he retorted, 'I could do with something myself. It's not every day I get mown down by a beautiful female. In fact, it has never happened to me before.'

His words mocked her a little and she was slightly puzzled by the enigmatic tone behind them, yet she was grateful that he wasn't thinking of abandoning her immediately.

'I'm sorry,' she exclaimed quickly, suddenly reminded, for all he chose to joke about it, that she might easily have caused a nasty accident. 'I should have been taking more care, not driving in such a hurry.'

'Forget it,' he dismissed her belated apology with a careless shrug of broad shoulders, and because he was obviously waiting for her to join him, she struggled to her feet. As she straightened, she was dismayed to find herself swaying, but before she could fall she was whipped up in a pair of strong arms and lowered bodily into his car.

'I don't know what came over me,' she protested weakly, as he got in beside her.

'Reaction,' he said briefly, leaning over to brush the tumbled dark hair from her face before fastening her seat belt.

Macy had forgotten about her seat belt and she glanced in some confusion at the dark face bending over her. Again the touch of his hands disturbed her. As he saw her watching him, a half smile appeared on his hard lips and she shrank instinctively, her turquoise eyes darkening with fear. From feeling warm and secure, she began to tremble, as every nerve in her body warned her against him.

His hands stayed on her waist. He might have been punishing her for her unconscious thoughts for a sudden coolness burned in his grey eyes. Macy stared into the dark face so near her own and gasped at the pressure of his fingers on her thigh. Her heart pounded violently as she realised she was entirely at his mercy then embarrassment flooded her as she became aware of how ridiculous she was being. Mutely she looked at him, her entreating glance full of silent remorse.

He took his time exploring her pale skin, the dark hair and brows, her long black lashes and trembling mouth. For a crazy moment she believed he was going to kiss her but instead, with a wry twist of his lips, he released her and switched the ignition of his car. 'So you decided to trust me, after all?'

Ashamed of herself, Macy nodded. Surprisingly she did. Here she was, going off with a man she had never seen before yet, despite her brief suspicions, she felt entirely safe. Manchester was a big city but she was sure he was a stranger to the area. If something about him stirred her deeply, there could be no lasting effect for after today she was unlikely to see him again. Once she managed to pull herself together she would be able to laugh at her own vulnerability.

Leaving the factory compound, the man stopped outside the hotel and helped her gently from the car to the lounge. After settling her comfortably in a quiet corner, he asked again how she was feeling. Something quivered through Macy as she heard him ordering drinks from a hovering waiter. Not for a long time could she remember anyone making a fuss over her like this.

He sat on the leather bench beside her and though she tried to relax she could feel his eyes constantly on her face. When the waiter returned with the brandy, he ordered coffee and sandwiches for her as well. 'You don't look as though you've had any lunch,' he said.

She hadn't, there hadn't been time, but she merely shook her head. 'I don't know why you're being so kind?'

'Don't you?' he murmured softly.

Again she shook her head, sudden tears stinging her eyes, forcing her to take an unsteady sip of the brandy he had placed in her hands.

'I'm thirty-four,' he said frankly, 'Young enough to find it easy to be kind to a beautiful girl.'

'So if I'd been old and ugly you wouldn't have bothered?' she accused tightly.

'Oh, I don't know,' he smiled. 'I would certainly have bothered but I mightn't have cared so much.'

She tried to be angry but didn't succeed, but when he raised one dark eyebrow she tried not to let his growing attraction distract her. She recognised in him a fundamental honesty but also a ruthless determination to have his own way that could be dangerous. His very nearness caused her to be nervous, uncertain of herself.

Taking another fortifying sip of brandy, she was grateful when the warmth of it began spreading through her veins. But as her strength returned, so did her senses. From being wonderfully dulled they became painfully sharp.

'My car!' she gasped, her smooth, oval face white again. 'I'll have to go back and see to it. I don't know what I could have been thinking of, just walking away and leaving it!'

Replacing her glass on the table with a thud, she jumped to her feet, only to find herself jerked back again by steely fingers.

'Calm down,' he advised curtly. 'I'll do everything that's necessary.'

'How can you?' she retorted wildly. 'I left the keys in. Someone might have stolen it by now!'

'I doubt it,' he laughed.

Mutinously she stared at him. 'I realise you think it funny but I can't manage without my car. Oh, please!' she began to struggle against his detaining hand. 'You don't understand! I have to go . . .'

'Calm down,' he repeated, this time more abrasively,

'I told you, I'll take care of it. If you can supply the number of the garage who usually does your servicing, I'll give them a ring and get them to collect it. It's as simple as that.'

A garage? Macy betrayed even more apprehension. 'I've only had the car a few weeks and it's never needed attention.'

He didn't appear to think there was anything odd about this, but, 'You must get your petrol somewhere?' he persisted. When she nodded blankly, he asked, 'Do you know if they do repairs?'

'I—I think so,' she stammered, feeling she was being tactfully manipulated through a series of questions like a child.

He stood up, raising his powerful frame to its full height with all the suppleness of a panther. 'Just give me their name and your own and it won't take a minute,' he promised.

'Macy,' she bit her lip uncertainly then amended quickly, 'Macy Gordon. The garage is Fultons, of Cross Street. I don't know the number.'

'No problem,' he smiled, adding more sternly before leaving her, 'Don't dare move before I get back.'

As he strode away from her, looking as if he was used to giving orders all his life, Macy gazed after him despairingly. As he had stared at her, imposing his will on her, her heart had begun pounding again. For some reason this man, who hadn't yet bothered to introduce himself, disturbed her. She was reacting to him all the time, like a puppet on a string. His nearness made her pulse race and her breath quicken as he aroused emotions she didn't understand and was instinctively afraid of. Many women would be content to describe him as tall, dark and handsome and to leave it at that. He was certainly all those things but so much more, she suspected, lay under the surface. From the top of his arrogantly held head to the toes of his expensively shod feet, he oozed an authority and power which made her shiver. He had told her not to move before he got back but she knew if she could have found a way of returning to the factory alone, she would have taken it.

He had asked her name without giving his and she wondered if he would tell her who he was? If he was just passing through he might think it irrelevant, yet if he was just passing through what had he been doing visiting the factory? When she considered the dozens of reasons why he might have been doing that, she smiled wryly at her own curiosity.

Trying not to think of how much her car might cost to repair, her slight smile faded to an unhappy frown. It wasn't so much a question of cost as how was she to manage without it? Her aunt had been terribly restless last night, Macy had got little sleep and Miss Kirby, her nurse, had been late in arriving this morning. If Macy hadn't had her car she would never have got to work on time. She used it frequently at lunch time, too, like today when she had dashed home to check up on her aunt and make sure Miss Kirby was coping.

The man returned, followed by his order for coffee and sandwiches. He resumed his seat as the waiter unloaded his tray and left them. Macy glanced at him warily. His mouth quirked slightly but his eyes, as they rested on her, were entirely sober. Again she was aware of his virility arousing sensations in her, much too alarming for her peace of mind.

'Did you get through to the garage?' she asked, abruptly forcing her thoughts to more mundane matters. She winced that it should be so difficult to concentrate on what must be nearly the most important thing she possessed.

'Yes,' his eyes, as before, never left her. 'They promised to see to it. You may only buy petrol from them but they appear to know who you are.'

'They do?'

'It seems so,' he replied, 'I just had to confirm it.'

'Confirm it?'

'You do have a flattering way of repeating things after me,' he teased. 'The chap I spoke to asked if Miss Gordon would be the girl with the long black hair and blue eyes and a Venus type figure?'

'Oh, please!' she protested, cheeks scarlet. So far as she was aware no one at the garage had taken much notice of her. 'You've been more than kind, Mr . . .?'

As she looked at him enquiringly, he smiled. 'Call me Brice.'

She wouldn't be seeing him again so what did a surname matter? Determined not to feel disappointed, she plunged on. 'I realise I've taken up quite a lot of your time already, er, Brice, and I'm afraid I'm going to have to ask you to run me back . . .'

'What's the hurry?' he cut in. 'You haven't had your coffee yet.' He began pouring it out.

One of his hands was holding the coffee pot, the other her. She couldn't move. 'My boss doesn't like his staff coming in at all hours.' She tried to wriggle her arm free of his fingers and failed.

'Humm.' Putting down the coffee pot, he laced her cup with sugar and milk, pushing it towards her along with the plate of sandwiches. She was suddenly so hungry she couldn't resist them.

'You work at the factory?'

The ham was delicious but it was suddenly tasteless as his light query somehow aroused all her old fears. 'I—I'm a textile designer,' she faltered.

'Ah, one of those?' Letting go of her aching arm, he thoughtfully stirred his own coffee before taking not one sandwich but two. He didn't carry an ounce of surplus flesh but Macy suspected his appetite would be large, for many things. She was flushing a little at the trend of her thoughts when he asked slowly, 'You enjoy being a textile designer?'

'Yes,' she began eagerly, until again she remembered and her small face clouded despairingly. Would the guilt and pain continue forever? She had no reason to believe it wouldn't. She digressed slightly. 'The factory has changed hands. We're all waiting for the new owner and a lot of people fear for their jobs.'

He appeared to hesitate for a moment, although Macy couldn't believe such an obviously decisive man would ever be uncertain over anything. 'A take-over can be worrying,' he said at last. 'A new management might make changes but that doesn't necessarily mean that jobs are at risk.'

'True,' she sighed, 'but it's an anxious time, all the same. There are bound to be changes.'

His grey eyes lit with the faint humour she was fast growing used to. 'You can't expect a new broom at least not to try and sweep clean?'

'People won't mind—if they have the freedom to work.'

'Yet sometimes that freedom is misspent,' he returned cynically.

Macy went so white that his eyes darkened in alarm and he called for more brandy. 'If you're worrying about being late for work,' he said tersely, 'forget it. I can't believe your supervisor is such a tyrant that he won't understand when you explain the circumstances.'

She let him think this was the reason for her distress but refused the brandy when it came. 'You're quite right, of course,' she whispered, 'Mr Paley isn't a tyrant. I'm just being silly.'

He frowned, as if something about her answer, for all he had suggested it himself, didn't satisfy him but he gave her a few moments to compose herself before he asked quietly. 'How long have you worked for Pearsons?'

'Just over a year.' Her hands clenched, thinking of the day she had started with all her high hopes, integrity and determination to give the firm who had been kind enough to take her on, all her loyalty. 'I was twenty-one.'

'You came straight out of art school?'

She nodded.

'So, what do you do exactly?'

Macy glanced at him uncertainly. Pearsons was a large concern, with factories scattered all over the Midlands and the north. Primarily they manufactured cloth which was sold to leading wholesalers and clothiers. But it was the exclusive designs they created for a number of leading couture houses that formed the most lucrative part of their business. These designs were naturally closely guarded secrets and no one employed in their creation was allowed to discuss them outside.

'I work in one of the specialist units,' she replied reluctantly.

His glance sharpened. 'I imagine a girl would need a lot of talent to get as far as that, at your age.'

Her voice faltered, though a faint colour touched her pale cheeks at his praise. 'I'm supposed to be very good but I'm not supposed to talk about it.'

'I can understand.'

To Macy's surprise, he seemed to approve for his silvery eyes warmed.

'So,' he smiled, 'you are a textile designer, twenty-two years of age, and you've lived in Manchester all your life?'

'Most of it,' she agreed.

'And you aren't married.' With a surprising tenseness his manner changed as he surveyed her ringless fingers. 'A boyfriend?'

She could have told him, I used to have, nothing serious but I used to go out with boys once. 'No,' she replied briefly instead.

'Fortunately for me.' He leaned nearer, taking her small hand in his larger one as he released a deep breath. 'Macy,' he said softly, 'will you have dinner with me this evening? I have to see you again.'

Macy went very still. Whether he lived in Manchester or was just passing through, it filled her with forbidden pleasure that he should want to. She wanted to see him again. She could feel the whole of her reaching out to him, which made it doubly difficult to tell him she couldn't.

'I'm sorry,' she whispered.

He frowned, his darkening gaze suggesting he might have resorted to violence but was striving to be reasonable. 'You said you haven't a boyfriend but perhaps you have other arrangements?'

'No, it's not that . . .' Her voice trailed off as she hesitated helplessly, suddenly afraid to tell him for it might mean revealing more than was wise, why she couldn't do as he asked. Yet finding it as impossible to invent an excuse, she stared at him frustratedly, unaware of the longing in her eyes.

'Macy?' His free hand came out to brush her cheek, allowing his thumb to trace lightly over her mouth. 'I can't let you refuse what I know we both want. I think you trust me and I promise you that trust is not misplaced.'

She was lost in the changing lights of his eyes. His thumb tormented her lips and a fierce longing she had never experienced before stormed through her. She had thought there couldn't be anything more important to her than her aunt but now she suspected she was mistaken. A slight tremor shook her as it struck her that if she refused to have dinner with this man she might never see him again. Would it be such a crime to give way to temptation just this once? If she asked Miss Kirby nicely she might agree to sit with Kate. Yet, staring at Brice anxiously, she wondered if it would be wise?

Aware of her uncertainty and seeking to dispel it, Brice Sinclair resorted to the ruthlessness which had served him so well all his life. As Macy quivered in his hands, he removed his exploring thumb from the curve of her lips and let his mouth take over. Expertly, in the empty lounge, he pulled her pliant body to the hardness of his and placing a hand behind her head, he covered her startled lips with his own. Her protests were silenced as his sensuous mouth began working a certain magic she found impossible to fight. The blood began burning through her veins, heightening her senses until she felt she must faint. The room swirled around her as Brice's arms tightened, as though they were both being consumed by the same thing. The desire to fight him passed and she longed to stay in his arms forever. He lifted his head to stare at her briefly and she sensed in him some kind of surprise before his mouth claimed hers again.

Then he released her, not hurriedly, he might have remembered where they were. His face was pale but he looked much more in control than she was. She recognised he would be able, with his greater experience, to hide his feelings better. She knew she ought to be glaring at him instead of staring at him with a kind of adolescent wonder in her eyes at the wildness of the ecstasy he had aroused inside her. Over the years she had been kissed by other men but none of their kisses had affected her like this.

While she was still gulping for air, he easily regained his lost composure. 'Has that helped you decide, Macy?'

Macy drew a shaking hand across her rumpled hair. 'Do you always get what you want, Brice?'

'I have to see you again,' he countered curtly. 'And you know that goes for you, too.' His grey eyes smouldered, 'Give me your address and I'll be there at seven-thirty.'

'But we've only just met!'

'What difference does it make how long we've known each other?'

They were making quick, tense conversation. Macy's soft lips quivered as she tried to concentrate her churning mind. Seven-thirty, he said. Eight would be better. This would give her time to arrange things with

Miss Kirby and to spend an hour with her aunt. What either of them would say, Macy had no idea—she hadn't been out of an evening since her aunt's condition had worsened. Aunt Kate wouldn't stand in her way, she was certain, but she might ask some difficult to answer questions. Whatever was happening to Macy was beyond her comprehension, but, whatever it was, it was encouraging in her a recklessness almost entirely foreign to her nature.

She raised eyes brightened to a brilliant blue to the man still bending over her. 'I live with my aunt and she hasn't,' Macy crossed her fingers unconsciously, 'been too well lately. I was home checking on her at lunch time, which was why I was hurrying. If I can get someone to stay with her this evening, I will have dinner with you, providing you promise to wait at the end of my road. If you come to the house and ring the bell, it could upset her.'

Brice nodded, consenting at last to drive her back to the factory. Ten minutes later she was back at her drawing board.

'I wish you'd let people know when you're going to be held up,' Thelma Brown, the department's second-in-command, noted sharply. 'Really, Macy, whenever George is away and I'm left in charge, I swear you take advantage!'

Macy flushed as the tartness of Thelma's voice struck her from behind. She turned slowly, trying to speak coolly. 'I'm sorry I'm late, Thelma, but I wasn't late deliberately. I didn't even know Mr Paley was going away.'

Thelma, a tall girl in her thirties, frowned as Macy's flush faded leaving her overly pale. 'There isn't anything wrong, is there . . .?' she asked, 'Your aunt . . .?'

'No,' Macy sighed. 'My aunt is no worse. The fact that I'm late is entirely my own fault. I was going too fast and had a slight collision at the factory gates.'

'Good heavens!' Thelma exclaimed, but looked more curious than sympathetic. 'What happened? Is your car damaged? Was anyone else involved?'

Macy bit her lip. It was more than probable that Thelma would discover what had happened from another source if she refused to enlighten her. It was amazing how difficult it was to hide anything that happened here. As Brice had lifted her into his car, and again, when he had dropped her off, someone was sure to have seen them. If not, the car park attendant must have noticed her damaged car.

'A man in a big black sports car, I think it was,' she murmured vaguely, answering Thelma's last question first. 'He managed to avoid me but I crashed into the wall and he took me to the William Hotel until I recovered from the shock.'

'Very—nice . . .!' Thelma drawled. 'Now why doesn't something like that ever happen to me?'

'I could have been hurt!' Macy pointed out quietly.

'But you weren't,' Thelma shrugged, staring at Macy impatiently. 'Well, for goodness sake, what was the man like? Was he young—good-looking? Nice?'

Brice was all those things, though the lines etched on his face betrayed that he had, long ago, left his extreme youth behind him. 'Yes,' she muttered reluctantly.

Thelma's inquisitive glance concentrated on the colour creeping under Macy's skin. Suspiciously she asked, 'Are you seeing him again?'

Why lie, or hide something she wasn't ashamed of? 'This evening,' she replied alloofly. 'Providing my aunt can manage without me.'

'My—you are a fast worker!' Thelma taunted sharply.

The colour in Macy's cheeks deepened but she lifted her chin. 'He asked me to have dinner with him and it would have seemed churlish to refuse after he had been so kind.'

'Had you seen him before today?' Thelma persisted,

as though determined to spoil Macy's pleasure if she could.

'No,' Macy confessed unhappily.

'Then are you sure you're being wise?' Thelma retorted, waspishly, 'After all, if he's a stranger...'

It was a question Macy might have found difficult to answer but thankfully Thelma was called away before she was forced to try.

Was she doing the right thing? Blindly Macy turned back to her work. Thelma was clearly doubtful while Macy suddenly had no doubts at all. Yet how could she have explained to Thelma or anyone, the fierce attraction which had sprung to life between Brice and herself? Her feelings for this stranger, like anything in the embryonic stage, if not properly cherished might fade and die. Certainly they might never be strong enough to withstand Thelma's ridicule.

Dismayed to find her hands trembling, Macy had to wait a few moments before resuming work on the delicate flower design she was constructing. Thelma knew too much already. It was Thelma who had tempted her to betray Pearsons and although she had never taken advantage of what Macy had done, Macy could never look at the other girl without feeling a sense of danger. Macy viewed her own part in the affair with increasing self-contempt. It was no use blaming Thelma entirely for what had happened. She'd had only to say no!

Thelma's brother was employed in a similar unit to this by another company in the south. Thelma, his junior by fifteen years, rarely saw him, but when he had been in danger of being made redundant she did rally round and do her best to help him. Apparently a competition was being held in his section, an award of two thousand pounds to be paid for the best design. Thelma, as aware as George Paley that Macy's work possessed a kind of magic, begged her to do something for her brother outside factory hours.

'You're his only chance,' she had appealed, catching Macy alone one day, after lunch. 'He has an invalid wife, just like your aunt, so you can understand how worried he is about losing his job. If he wins this award, no one will dream of making him redundant and, more important perhaps for you, he promises he will pay you half the prize money. You would get a thousand pounds! Just think what you could do for your aunt with that.'

At first Macy was so shocked and disgusted at Thelma's suggestion that she should not only betray her employer but break all the rules, that she had refused to countenance such an idea. Macy's family might never have had any money but she had been brought up to recognise a sense of loyalty. It was the thought of Thelma's brother's wife and her aunt which had eventually influenced her decision. With a heavy heart she had realised the choice wasn't really hers. Because of what Kate had done for her, wasn't she duty bound to try and repay her—and this might be her last chance? Her first consideration must be to her aunt before the factory and her own conscience.

Since her mother had died when Macy was born, Kate Gordon, her father's sister, had brought her up. Strictly, perhaps, but she had been the only mother Macy had known. If it hadn't been for Kate, what would have happened to her?

Macy's father, a scholar and a dreamer, had spent his time writing scholarly books which, although published, rarely brought in more than a pittance. Just as soon as Macy was old enough to be left, Kate had resumed her secretarial work and without her salary they might have starved. She had put Macy through art school, recognising her niece's talent almost as soon as she was able to draw. Then, as often happens, just when everything appeared to be going right, everything began going wrong.

Macy's father had died suddenly and Kate was struck

down with a terminal illness. At first she had fought it with the courage she had always displayed, but it had advanced too swiftly. She had spent weeks in hospital but her dearest wish had been to come home. It had never been mentioned to her that they could be her last days but Macy suspected she knew.

The problem was Kate needed someone with her, or at least near at hand, all the time. As there were no savings financing this was impossible. If Macy gave up her job to look after her, Kate's invalidity allowance would never stretch to cover the high rent and keep the two of them, especially as Kate required so much extra if she was to live out her last days in any kind of comfort. What was really necessary was a nurse but Macy's earnings were scarcely enough to cover household expenses never mind such a luxury as that.

The money Thelma had offered had therefore proved too great a temptation. Macy had worked on the design in her spare time and Thelma's brother had won the design award with it. She had received a thousand pounds which paid for Miss Kirby, a redundant trained nurse, to come in and be with her aunt while she was at work. The car Macy ran had been sold to her by a neighbour. She had let Macy have it for a hundred pounds. It had belonged to her late husband and she said this was the highest price she had been offered. The car was an enormous help as it enabled Macy to leave home later in the morning and to be back much earlier than she could otherwise have been.

It was a great load off Macy's mind to know that Kate was being properly looked after. Nevertheless, if she had known the overwhelming feelings of guilt that were to follow, she doubted if she would ever have done what she had done. There were nights when she couldn't sleep, or when she woke, drenched in sweat, as reminders of her own treachery returned even through the darkness to haunt her. She had been so busy concentrating on what she could do with the money that she had missed considering the psychological aspects. She was a thief who had betrayed those who trusted her and she found the knowledge impossible to live with. After her aunt no longer needed her, she had vowed she would go and see Mr Pearson and confess the whole sorry story. And when Mr Pearson died she resolved that, when the time came, she would make the same confession to whoever took over, even if it meant instant dismissal or worse. For a crime such as she had committed, Macy suspected she might easily get a prison sentence.

She finished at five. Mr Paley was back and Thelma had been too busy to ask any more awkward questions. Just as she was leaving, Mr Paley called her over.

'Someone's ordered a taxi for you, Macy. Driver's just called to say he's waiting by the main gates.'

'A—taxi?' Macy's eyes widened, 'Are you sure?'

'Surprised, are you?' George Paley's teasing laughter rumbled, 'So was I child. Living it up, aren't you? Where's your car?'

As it appeared Thelma hadn't mentioned it, Macy again related what had happened but missing out most of the details this time. She merely told George that she had been careless and that her car was off the road. She wasn't sure what to make of the taxi. Despite a faint uneasiness, a glow of appreciation touched her heart as she thought of Brice, for the taxi could only have come from him. It was nice of him to do this for her. Somehow, she'd had a horrid suspicion, that after he had dropped her off that afternoon, he would forget all about her—along with their dinner date.

Wishing George a smiling good night, she hurried from the building, feeling happier than she had done in a long time. For once she refused to let doubts swamp her. Doubts like most things having to be paid for, eventually!

CHAPTER TWO

'YOU'RE sure you don't mind, darling?' Macy enquired of her aunt. She had asked not once but several times if her aunt minded her going out, and a hint of wry amusement briefly eased the lines which pain had worn on Kate Gordon's face.

She glanced at her niece affectionately. 'Why don't you stop fussing, dear, and just go? No one's going to run away with me and it's about time you had some fun. It's not natural for a girl of your age to be at home every evening.'

Macy started to frown then smiled instead. Kate hated being fussed over. It disturbed her almost as much as suspecting she was the reason why Macy stayed at home so much. Macy usually teased that she had only to ask Miss Kirby to baby-sit, but the truth was that she gained little pleasure from going anywhere with her aunt so ill. And it would have been cruel to say to Kate that there would be plenty of time to go anywhere she wished, when she was no longer here.

'How do you think I look?' The smile faded from Macy's sweetly curved lips as she awaited her aunt's verdict. Her black hair gleamed with blue lights and a light covering of make-up enhanced her white skin and blue eyes. The red model dress she was wearing, which she had picked up in a sale after she had first started working, clung seductively to her slender young figure, and the necklace she had fastened round her long graceful neck looked fabulous with it and much more expensive than it had actually been.

'Wonderful, dear!' Kate's reply might have been brief but there was a great warmth of feeling behind that one word. She added, with just a trace of anxiety, 'I'd rather you'd arranged to meet your young man here though. I should have liked to have met him. I can't say that I approve of your arrangements to meet at the end of the street. Are you sure you'll be all right?'

'Of course!' Macy laughed deliberately. She had told both Kate and Miss Kirby that she was having dinner with a man she had met at the factory. It might be a slight distortion of the truth but Kate would have worried, more than she was doing now, if she had revealed exactly what had happened. Instead of telling her about the accident and how her car was going to take at least thirty, difficult to spare, pounds to repair, she had pretended it had gone in for servicing.

'I mentioned, remember, that I wasn't sure about Miss Kirby. And if I couldn't get out I didn't want him hanging around.'

'You could have given him supper if Miss Kirby had been unable to stay,' Kate said reproachfully. 'You know I wouldn't have minded you having him in and you could have played records in the lounge.'

Macy had thought of this but rejected the idea. For some obscure reason she didn't want Brice to know about her aunt. Not how ill she was, anyway. It could all be wrapped up with her guilt regarding what she had done but she feared it was more likely to be the reluctance she felt to let him get too close. After tonight their paths weren't likely to cross again. If she'd asked him to the house, even if he hadn't met Kate, he might have taken it as a hint that she would welcome the kind of intimacy she wasn't yet ready to cope with. Unhappily she glanced at Kate. Hadn't she enough heartache already without that!

Re-pinning the smile on her lips, she bent quickly and kissed Kate's gaunt cheek. 'When I get to know him better, darling, I promise to bring him to see you.'

A promise which would never be fulfilled, she thought wistfully, as she assured Miss Kirby she wouldn't be late. Miss Kirby, like Kate, was always urging Macy to get out more, but Macy knew that Miss Kirby, however willing, couldn't work twenty-four hours a day. She needed her rest, like everyone else, and someone must always be on hand for when Kate required attention. Kate was a model patient, undemanding and uncomplaining, but with the best will in the world, there were things she could no longer do for herself.

Macy worked in the industrial belt which spread out north of Manchester. She lived ten miles away on the edge of the city. The street she lived in was lined on either side by semi-detached houses, all depressingly similar. Brown windows complemented brown or green doors and often a twitching curtain was the only sign of life. When she was younger, Macy had dreamed of living in the country and though she had long since lost all hope of her dream coming true, she had, until her aunt had taken ill, spent most of her spare time exploring the countryside. The unspoiled moors were never far away and she never grew tired of them.

Brice was waiting at the end of the street, exactly as she had asked him to. His sleek black car, gleaming like a monster through the darkness, made the few other vehicles parked nearby appear nondescript by comparison. She was so busy looking at it that she didn't see Brice standing a few yards away and whirled in panic when he spoke.

'Macy?' In two strides he was beside her, his arm going out to steady her. 'Did I give you a fright?'

'It's becoming a habit,' she quipped, hoping the forced lightness of her voice would hide how she was trembling. What was it about this man, she wondered apprehensively, that could reduce her to a jelly-like mass in seconds?

'I'm sorry.' His mouth quirked as he settled her in the black car. 'It does look that way, doesn't it? Actually, I was trying to get a breath of fresh air. Apart from when I saw you, I've been gradually smothering all afternoon in a . . . er . . . room where the heating was too high.'

She wondered what he had been doing all afternoon, after he had left her, but he didn't say. When he got in beside her, she said politely, 'Thank you for the taxi. It saved me a tiring journey.'

'I checked on your car and told them to get on with it,' he replied.

She guessed from his tone that she wouldn't be long without it thanks to his intervention. When she rang the garage they had refused to promise anything. She sighed that men could still succeed where women failed.

'You're very kind,' she murmured, swallowing her resentment.

He turned to look at her in the half darkness. 'Even in this light I can see how beautiful you are,' he said huskily, 'I didn't know how you would be feeling but thank you for coming.'

'If I hadn't,' she replied, as huskily, 'I mightn't have seen you again.'

His hand lifted to a switch and the inside of the car was suddenly illuminated with bright light. As Macy blinked, he studied her face closely. There was an odd tenseness about him, an excitement in his grey eyes that he didn't try and hide. Macy wondered at it as she tried to return his exploratory glance calmly. Something told her that excitement was an emotion quite foreign to him. One he seldom experienced.

Unlike herself, he wasn't wearing an overcoat and she saw how his dark jacket covered his broad shoulders as if it had been purposely tailored to fit them. Letting her eyes wander further, she realised his evening dress certainly hadn't come off a peg. Whoever Brice was, his car and clothes proclaimed he wasn't a man short of money.

'Hello!' he said softly.

Macy lifted her eyes to his glowing ones and knew this was no ordinary greeting. He spoke like someone who had found something he had been searching for for a long time. Macy gasped then swiftly clamped down on the thought that Brice's mysterious air of triumph could have anything to do with her. This evening, she was conscious again of his vitality but also of his dark and dangerous sophistication. A man like this would have no serious use for a young inexperienced girl like herself. She was helping him pass what might otherwise have been a lonely, boring evening in a strange town. Nothing more. Tomorrow she would almost certainly be forgotten when he moved on.

Bleakly she gazed at him, despair clouding her eyes and stiffening her limbs.

'Macy!' he growled reproachfully, and suddenly she was forgetting the nonsense she had been thinking and smiling at him.

'Oh, Brice,' she whispered tremulously. 'Somehow I didn't believe you'd be here. I couldn't work this afternoon for thinking of you.'

Grasping her wrist, so he was bound to feel her racing pulse, he lifted her hand to hold it over his heavily beating heart. 'I thought of nothing else,' he confessed. 'I couldn't concentrate either. I was going out of my mind. I saw more than one person looking at me.'

She had never felt a man's heart thudding against her fingers before, nor had her palms ever been prickled by the hairs on a man's chest from under the fine cotton of his shirt. For the sake of her sanity, before the sensations surging through her merged completely in the approaching gleam of his eyes, she forced herself to draw away from him.

Surprisingly he let her go. He might have taken pity on her obvious struggle for breath for his own breathing had altered subtly. He stared at her for a few more seconds, as though imprinting her features on his memory before turning away.

As they drove off he steered the conversation to more normal channels. 'I trust your aunt is feeling better too? Did you tell her about me?'

'I wanted to.' Macy glanced at him uncertainly. 'I'm afraid I had to be a bit vague for fear she asked your full name. She would never have approved if I'd been forced to confess I didn't know it.'

'Sinclair,' he muttered, so absently she decided she had imagined the slight pause.

'Sinclair . . .?' she repeated thoughtfully.

'Rings a bell, does it?'

She saw his hand tense on the wheel and wondered at his cynical tones. 'No,' she replied. 'At least,' she frowned, 'I'm not sure. I seem to have heard the name somewhere, lately, but there must be other Sinclairs around.'

'I can't be the only one,' he agreed tersely.

'Have I said something I shouldn't?' she faltered as his face darkened.

The corner of his hard mouth quirked. 'I'm sorry, Macy. I've had a bit of a day.'

Was he blaming her? He had said he'd found it difficult to concentrate but she couldn't have been responsible for his mind wandering that much? He had checked up on her car. Maybe it was really his conscience that had been troubling him? It wasn't possible to be influenced to that extent by someone you had just met!

Macy clenched her hands into fists. That last thought concerned herself as much as Brice. She must have fallen for him in the first few minutes. As she suddenly realised this her whole body stiffened in unconscious reaction. She felt she was developing a fever from an unknown virus she had no resistance to. The only thing clear in her mind was that she had to fight it. She had learned that the man by her side was called Sinclair. He was thirty-four, tall dark and arrogant, which probably meant he had his fair share of pride. In personality, he was decisive and commanding, but what he did, or exactly who he was she had yet to discover. Macy drew a sharp breath as suddenly and unpredictably, all her senses warned her against any further involvement with him.

The night was dark, winter being reluctant to make way for spring, which usually came late to the north, anyway. As a shower of rain hit the windscreen and the powerful wipers sprang into immediate action, she shivered.

Brice hadn't spoken for a while, now he muttered caustically. 'Whatever it is you've been working out, you don't appear to find your conclusions comforting.'

A hard surge of feeling knotted her stomach as he turned his dark head to glance at her. She had thought he was busy mulling over his disappointing day. 'I suppose you've guessed what I was thinking about?'

'You and me the way we met. You're feeling mixed up.'

Disturbed would be more applicable. She flushed and was glad he couldn't see inside her head. 'You could put it like that,' she murmured.

'Are you like your aunt?' he asked suddenly.

Macy glanced at him in surprise. 'Why?'

'You said she wouldn't approve of your going out with a stranger, which tells me quite a lot about how you've been brought up. If she brought you up?'

'She did.' At this stage, Macy didn't mention her father. He had always been too wrapped up in his books to bother about what she was doing. 'Kate was strict,' she mused, 'but she used to say I needed a firm hand.'

Brice laughed gently and covered her hand with his. He didn't grope, as some men did, he went for his target with a sureness that hinted at another facet of his character. 'I think your aunt and I will get along fine,' he said softly.

'She's all the family I have,' Macy said unhappily.

Slanting a quick glance at her suddenly strained face, Brice continued in the same tone. 'One day soon, Macy, we have to talk about your family and I'll tell you about mine, but first I want to get to know you.'

'You might not like me when you do.'

'I already like you,' he pointed out. 'I can't see how getting to know each other better is going to alter that.'

Didn't he? A hollow laugh, quickly smothered, rose in Macy's throat. She had believed he was just passing through but he talked as though this wasn't the case. If he stayed and they saw more of each other, what would he say if he ever discovered she was a thief? It didn't take much imagination to guess.

When she didn't reply, Brice's grip tightened on her taut fingers. 'Macy,' he exclaimed. 'What's wrong? You're reacting all the time but it's to something in yourself, not me. There might be some connection but I'm not what's worrying you. I think it's something more fundamental. Can't you tell me?'

He was too astute! Staring at the headlights of passing cars, she avoided a direct answer. 'Why should I confide in you?' she muttered. 'You're a stranger.'

He ignored this, as if it wasn't worthy of the breath she had used. 'Was there trouble when you were late back from lunch?'

'No,' she replied quickly. 'My boss doesn't tolerate slackness but he isn't that bad. Anyway, he was out all afternoon.'

'You told him why you were late?'

'Not—everything.'

He laughed and squeezed her hand. 'Not—everything could be told . . .'

'No . . .' A wondering expression lit Macy's eyes as she marvelled at the way they seemed to be exactly on the same wavelength. The feeling that lay between them would be difficult to explain to anyone. What would Thelma or Kate have said if she'd confessed that the man she had just met filled her with emotions she had never known existed? The sensation creeping up her arm now, as their hands touched, was burning through her body in a way she would never have believed possible. She quivered as she wondered convulsively how she would feel if Brice were to stop the car, take her in his arms and make love to her?

His voice intruded on her chaotic thoughts, startling her. 'There you go again,' he sighed. 'Shivering!'

Macy almost jumped. Again she was thankful, as embarrassment flooded her, that he couldn't read her thoughts. He might come close to it but in this instance she was relieved that he couldn't know exactly what she was thinking. He spoke carelessly but she noticed his jaw was tense, as if, though he pretended to tease, her reactions were important to him.

'I—it was cold walking down the street,' she stammered. 'I'm still not warm.'

They both knew this was an excuse but Brice didn't make an issue of it. Silently he turned up the car heating and concentrated on the increasing traffic as they skirted the city centre.

'Have you been to Manchester before?' Macy asked when he parked outside one of the leading hotels. For a stranger he knew his way around remarkably well. Coming from her area, he had never once taken a wrong turning or asked for advice.

'Once or twice,' he replied briefly. 'I have a photographic memory for city streets, if that's what you're wondering about. It makes travelling a lot easier.'

Should that contain a clue as to what he did? 'You're lucky,' she rejoined dryly, hiding her curiosity.

The hotel was busy but a table was found for them in a quiet alcove. To Macy's surprise, the maitre d'hotel appeared to know Brice well, he escorted them over to their table himself. He addressed Brice as Mr Sinclair and certainly didn't skimp on the deferential treatment. Macy felt like a princess and marvelled that Brice wasn't similarly impressed. Obviously he was much more used to this kind of thing than she was. She wondered suspiciously if this was where he was staying and dismissed the notion that he was a salesman.

'You look beautiful,' he said when they were alone.

Macy felt annoyed with herself when she flushed. She was sure the pink in her cheeks must match her dress as Brice's appreciative glance searched over her. As his eyes rested on her breasts, her colour deepened and her heart began racing.

'Thank you,' she replied, trying to speak lightly in order to hide her confusion. 'I expect you say that to all the women you take out.'

His glance narrowed as he met her faintly challenging eyes. 'You sound as if you don't believe me, yet other men must have told you how beautiful you are.'

Without meaning to, she retorted sharply. 'None of my previous escorts have gone in for outrageous flattery.'

His mouth went so grim she immediately felt ashamed. 'How many others have there been, I wonder?'

'Not many.'

His dark brows rose savagely. 'I'm asking about your lovers.'

She had been about to retort, none, but she realised that Brice might not believe her. She was a virgin and hoped to stay that way until she fell in love with someone deeply enough to give herself to him. But such views, today, were considered old-fashioned and more often held in ridicule rather than respect.

'Don't worry,' Brice said tightly when, despite the indifferent shrug she managed, her brow pleated slightly, 'I'm not inexperienced myself so I'm scarcely in a position to criticise.'

Staring down at the tablecloth, Macy found herself wondering about the women he had made love to. To her dismay, as a tremor of something very like jealousy shook her, she found herself asking impulsively. 'D-do you enjoy making love?'

His mouth twisted cynically. 'Once I thought it one of the few pleasures in life.'

'And—now?'

He smiled thinly at the look of half-eager revulsion on her face. 'You're asking a lot of questions, aren't you, for a girl who's experienced herself? I presume you're after my personal opinion on the matter?' When she nodded dully, he said dryly, 'I think I'm coming to realise that there might be more to making love than just sex.'

Macy was aware that every word he spoke was accelerating her heart-beats, as if he was applying them directly to herself. 'Do you usually hold such intimate conversations with strangers, Mr Sinclair?'

His eyes gleamed with faint amusement at her obvious attempt to put some distance between them. 'Didn't you help to instigate it, Macy?' he smiled. When she nodded unhappily, he added more sternly, 'I don't intend that we should remain strangers, my dear, but maybe I am taking too many hurdles too fast? It might be a better idea to start at the beginning and take things from there. I've learned a little about you so don't you want to know about me? Where I come from, what I'm doing here, how long I intend staying?'

Again she knew the inexplicable fear of involvement that she had experienced earlier. 'No!' she panicked, paling, 'I—I'm not really curious about you, and ... well, I mean, does it matter?'

'Not immediately.' He frowned, his eyes resting on her face, more interested in the cause of her agitation. 'You'll have to know one day but that's entirely up to you. I have no particular wish to relate a lot of boring details. As long as you don't believe I'm hiding anything underhand or contemptible.'

Macy bowed her head so he wouldn't notice her cheeks growing colder. How was it that every now and then he said something more applicable to herself than to him. She had only begged fate for one night but what chance did she stand of enjoying even a few minutes of it?

'I thought you were just passing through,' she confessed hollowly. 'I thought you had asked me out because like most people in a strange town you were lonely. When I accepted your invitation I believed it was the least I could do, after what you'd done for me.'

'Shall I tell you something?' he said so curtly it jerked up her head. As their eyes met and she swallowed, he continued remorselessly. 'I am a stranger in this town, but I am acquainted with a few people who would have been only too happy to have kept me company this evening. So that dispenses with the reason why you think I asked you out. As for your own motives? I'm not sure that I appreciate your agreeing to dine with me out of gratitude. If I was certain that was your sole reason I might slap you.'

He would, too! A faint cold brushed over her as she stared at him apprehensively. She wanted to tell him that gratitude was only one of the emotions she felt, but if she told him this what might she be betraying? If she confessed to all the emotions swarming through her—if she could put a name to them—every time he looked at her, he might easily think she was offering herself to him? Or worse, he might get the impression that she was a girl used to picking up strange men and leading them on, having affairs with them. After all, she wasn't that young!

Meeting the coolness of his icy glance she decided confrontation might be the best form of retreat. 'I—I suppose you're the sort who beats his wife?'

For some reason this amused him. He clearly relaxed. 'I wouldn't beat you all the time,' he promised. 'Just when you deserved it.'

She returned his smile although hers wobbled slightly as he went on gazing at her intently, as though the joke he had made had started up a train of thought in his mind. As if he couldn't see enough of her, his eyes roamed over her, his recent anger forgotten.

'You're so perfect,' he groaned. 'I wonder where you've been all my life. Why didn't I come back four years ago? What a lot of time we might have saved.'

Macy was saved from answering or having to make any comment by the arrival of their meal. As a waiter and wine waiter hovered until Brice dismissed them Macy smoothed her napkin over her lap. She was on edge and Brice knew it. He was still going too fast for her but he seemed to have forgotten he had promised to slow down. A look of intense excitement kept flickering across his face and it was obvious that he was looking for a similar response in herself. There was at times a look of ruthless determination about him. He was deliberately stirring up her emotions and making it clear he wasn't going to stop.

She began eating, needing time to quieten the turmoil inside her, to re-establish her usual calm. Any kind of composure was difficult to maintain near the man sitting opposite her but for her own sake she had to try. In between bites she was unconsciously pausing to take long deep breaths, as if searching for a strength she couldn't find.

Brice, as though willing to be patient with her, talked lightly throughout the meal on general topics—which was just as well for Macy didn't find herself capable of more than an occasional monosyllabic reply. She tried to eat but every mouthful threatened to choke her and she was unable to do full justice to a meal which she recognised to be as delicious as it was expensive.

The unsteadiness of her pulse increased as she met Brice's enigmatical eyes. How was it possible to feel so much for someone one scarcely knew? It frightened her more than a little to realise that if she saw much more of him she could be in danger of falling in love. The beat of her heart warned her that she was halfway there already and the only safe thing to do might be never to see him again.

When she was sure she couldn't force down another

morsel, she laid down her pudding spoon and the waiter came to remove their plates.

Brice ordered coffee in the lounge without consulting her.

'I won't have to be late,' she protested, amazed to discover, on glancing at her watch, how long they had lingered over dinner.

'So it's no use asking you to my room?' he teased.

He couldn't be serious! Macy argued with herself that he couldn't be while their coffee was being served. With a plan to drink her coffee fast and leave, she almost scalded her tongue.

'Careful,' Brice warned.

Wasn't she trying to be! 'Do you intend staying here long?' she asked impulsively.

'That depends,' he replied quietly. 'Probably not forever but I expect to be in Manchester for some time.'

Macy had sworn she wouldn't ask. She wished now that she hadn't as predictably a shudder ran through her.

Brice stirred his coffee thoughtfully then looked straight at her. 'Macy,' he said, 'I realise, despite what you said before dinner, that you must have your normal share of curiosity. You must be wondering about me.'

'No!' she exclaimed, as she had then, irrational fears not allowing her to act normally. What sort of chance would any kind of relationship between them stand when she was so loaded down with guilt and had so much to repay and put right? Brice would undoubtedly meet someone else and remember her with a quirk of humour. It was the best she could hope for.

She looked back at him, a hint of strain in her eyes. 'We're strangers, Brice. I don't see any need for heart to heart talks. If you are staying in Manchester, you mentioned there are people you know. I'm sure there must be a woman among them willing to help to amuse you sometimes.'

'That must be the speech of the century,' he mocked,

eyes glinting. 'I've never had to beg when I've wanted a woman in my bed, if that's what you're hinting at. But I never have time to indulge myself that much.'

He wasn't sparing her blushes but maybe she deserved to feel hot all over. 'You might be married,' she mumbled.

His mouth twisted. 'You said you weren't curious?'

Awkwardly she retorted, 'That's only one question.'

Brice laughed mockingly. 'The first of many, don't you mean? And the answer is no, I'm not married. So far I've escaped the net though I've a feeling that my luck has run out. Anything more?'

'No.' Her eyes flickered nervously as she wondered what he meant about his luck running out? 'I think we are destined to be ships that pass in the night, Mr Sinclair.'

His laughter faded to a frown and he regarded her long and thoroughly, almost insolently. He could be punishing her for her lack of co-operation and she shrivelled under his narrowed stare and the hardness of his tones when he spoke. 'You're a beautiful girl, Macy Gordon, and I want to see more of you. If you'd rather not know about me—that's fine by me, but we won't be ships that pass in the night, that I can assure you. We're going to be seeing a lot of each other, you and I, and one thing's for certain, I'm going to have you before we part company, if ever we do.'

Macy would have leapt up and fled, like a frightened doe if his hand hadn't shot out to clamp her down. He was angry and she was scared. It wasn't a mixture to cool ruffled feelings as they stared at each other.

Glaring at him, Macy exclaimed, 'You can't expect me to stay here when you're threatening to—to seduce me, like that!'

He smiled, the taunting, teeth-bared smile of the hunting tiger. 'You'll be willing enough when the time comes. I don't contemplate having to use more force than any of your other lovers. There's something between us that's too strong to ignore, and as the feeling is mutual why try to deny it? You must have had pleasure from the company of other men. I would see to it that you got a great deal more pleasure from mine.'

Macy was so furiously disappointed she could have wept. He was being deliberately insulting. 'I thought you liked me?' she cried.

'Perhaps I'm trying not to?' Self-mockery edged his voice. 'You aren't the only one who could be taking fright.'

She could understand this. He was probably a busy man who could well do without problems in his personal life. It was time they both began being sensible and Brice might thank her for taking the lead.

Shaking off his detaining hand, she stood up. Swallowing the remnants of her temper, she said, 'I really have to go now, Brice. I promised my aunt I wouldn't be late.'

This time he didn't argue. Without a word he signed a chit for their meal then guided her outside to his car. He looked impatient rather than angry with her but she thought if he was, and didn't want to see her again, it might be the best thing that could happen. He had her so mixed up it wasn't comfortable. One moment she was riding recklessly on waves of incredible happiness, the next she was full of painful doubts, her spirits sinking lower by the minute. If she went on like this she feared for the eventual state of her mind. It might never stand such an insidious battering.

Brice drew up at the end of the street, exactly where he had met her. 'Shall I leave the car here?' he asked, 'and walk the rest of the way with you, or am I allowed to run you to your door?'

'This will do nicely, thank you,' Macy smiled, not quite meeting his eyes. 'And I don't need to be escorted further. You've done enough for one night.'

'Humm,' he appeared to be considering her rather veiled statement. 'You enjoyed being with me?'

He wasn't making it easy but she didn't try and avoid the truth. 'Yes, I did,' she confessed weakly.

Surprising her, he slid his hands to her waist, raising them until they stopped just under the fullness of her breasts. Something flared in his eyes as he bent towards her. 'Kiss me good night,' he said huskily.

Before she could summon strength to refuse him, his mouth touched hers, gently at first. There was still time to draw back but once he kissed her she was lost. Her lips parted of their own volition as he began kissing the delicate softness of her mouth.

When her brief restraint lessened and she responded eagerly, he wrapped both arms around her to lift her across him, pressing her slender body firmly against the stirring hardness of his. Macy was crushed against the breadth of his chest and gasped in sudden fear as she became aware of her violent heartbeats which she was sure Brice must feel. Belatedly she tried to fight him, at the same time attempting to clear her rapidly clouding senses and to strengthen a resistance he was fast overcoming. His head lifted but only far enough to allow his smouldering eyes to examine her trembling mouth, the colour fluctuating under her exquisite skin, the general state of disorientation he had reduced her to in seconds. Then with a groan he covered her lips with his again, ending all her attempts to reject him.

Without relinquishing her mouth, Brice slowly unbuttoned her coat, to allow him closer access to the curves it covered. His hand moved from gently caressing the exposed skin at the nape of her neck to slide warmly across her bare shoulders before settling at the low curve of her back. There he pressed her more closely against him, so she could feel the response of his hardening muscle.

When she moaned softly as the passion between them increased, he took no notice. His mouth continued devouring hers hotly until it seemed she would become one with his unrelenting hardness. The heat of his body merged with her own, causing her to melt into him. Her fingers fluttered helplessly to his face, seeking the hard planes of it before creeping upwards to thread through his thick dark hair. She felt she was being consumed by the intensity of emotion sweeping through her as the feeling between them leapt ever higher.

Then, as he had done in the hotel that afternoon, when he had kissed her, Brice drew sharply back. There was heat in his face, she saw, as her eyes fluttered open and she stared at him. Her own face felt hot. She could feel the blood in he cheeks and knew she was flushed. Her body didn't seem to belong to her any more. Even her voice sounded strange as she bemusedly whispered his name.

She had no means of knowing whether he had heard her for he made no reply but went on regarding her with a kind of burning intensity in his eyes. At last he said huskily, as she still trembled against him, 'What am I going to do with you, my sweet? We can't go on like this but I have to see you again.'

CHAPTER THREE

STILL at the mercy of feelings she had never experienced before, Macy nodded blindly. All her senses were alive but concentrating almost wholly on the incredible delight that had consumed her when Brice had kissed her. She couldn't seem to think of anything else but she tried to pull herself together for fear he could read her mind.

Drawing a deep breath, she lowered her long lashes in an instinctive attempt to hide her humiliating transparency. Feebly she attempted to extricate herself from his arms but although he wasn't rough with her, he wouldn't allow it. Turning her averted face back to him, he kissed her gently, his passion tightly leashed.

'I'm not rejecting you,' he muttered huskily. 'I want to make love to you, only not like this. I've never made love in a car and I don't intend to start now.'

'It's too soon, anyway,' Macy whispered, bewilderment darkening her eyes. 'Too sudden . . .'

'I've come to believe, in the last few hours,' Brice said tersely, 'that with some people things happen suddenly or not at all.'

'W-what kind of things?' she stammered nervously.

Self-derision edged the smile he gave her. 'It's not difficult to explain, my sweet,' he shrugged. 'Even if it isn't as easy to understand. Two people meet and immediately know they have to belong to each other. It's known as instant attraction, something I've always been sceptical about, yet as soon as I saw you it happened to me before I had a chance to defend myself.'

Meeting the cool mockery in his eyes, Macy still wasn't sure what he was talking about, or whether to take him seriously. He was frank but his manner was slightly guarded and he spoke of possession and wanting, rather than love. She had always thought it was love at first sight that happened to people—the kind of attraction Brice described seemed to have more to do with sex!

'There must be something between us,' she admitted slowly, 'but I don't know that we'd be wise to take much notice of it.'

He frowned, the wariness in his eyes replaced by a hint of impatience. 'There are some things you have to take notice of, Macy. I'm sorry if it frightens you but I want you and mean to have you.'

As her eyes widened, he gave her a mocking smile which did nothing but confirm his intentions. Yet despite a fleeting apprehension, Macy's heart began beating rapidly again with excitement. She wanted him too. Why couldn't she be as honest as he was and admit it? When he kissed her the rest of the world faded. He was becoming like a drug she couldn't do without. In his arms she no longer remembered her guilt which turned every conscious moment into something torturous to be lived through. This man's kisses could, amazingly, blot out all that. How could she give him up?

Again he kissed her with surprising gentleness but when she would have clung to him passionately, he resisted. Evidence that he didn't resist her easily showed in the iron grip of the hands he used to transfer her from his arms back into the passenger seat. 'Don't tempt me any more,' he growled. 'Otherwise I might forget where I am and do something we might both regret.'

Macy felt cold even after he gently eased the straps of her dress back on her shoulders and carefully fastened her coat. With only a few inches of space between them common sense returned painfully. She was throwing herself at a man she had known merely hours! Where was her strict upbringing, her aunt's love and trust? Her own, until now, easily applied principles?

Suddenly she felt sick and ashamed, entirely miserable. 'I'm sorry,' she began.

'Don't be,' he silenced her swiftly, decisively. 'The last thing I want you to be, Macy, is full of remorse. All I'm trying to say is, if you want me to take it slowly, you have to help. It's not going to help either of us if you're going to be continually worrying.'

She nodded quickly, shyness and a sudden gratitude in her glance. 'I have to go now.'

'Good girl,' he smiled. 'That's a good, old-fashioned remark I've never appreciated before tonight.'

She asked hesitantly as they walked along the street. 'You've been out with a lot of women?'

Recognising the doubt in her voice, his hand tightened on her arm. 'I'm nearly thirty-five, Macy. I can't deny there have been a few but you're the first one I've ever felt desperate about seeing again. The others mean nothing.'

Did he expect her to believe that? 'Why did you take them out in the first place?' she taunted, 'If you couldn't care less about them?'

'Mostly to relieve a very masculine urge,' he replied coolly, as if inclined to punish her for asking such foolish questions.

Mortified she hung her head, her cheeks scarlet. She was acting childishly and deserved his censure but she hadn't been prepared for him to be quite so blunt! 'I'm sorry,' she apologised.

'Macy!' he paused to swing her round, not over gently, his eyes glittering into her wide, upraised ones through the darkness. 'You're either very innocent or a very good actress. I've been no saint in the past. I've made love to women but I don't think I've broken many hearts. Does the same apply to you?'

What was he saying—asking? Macy frowned, too tired to try and work it out. 'It's late, Brice,' she tried to avoid his searching glance. 'You'll have to excuse me. I'd better go in, honestly.'

His mouth tightened and she thought he was going to insist that she answered him properly but he relented.

'I have to go to London tomorrow, Macy. I'll be back the next day and I want you to have dinner with me.'

Two days seemed like a life-time! 'Yes,' she replied simply, not even wondering how she was going to manage it.

'I'll pick you up at eight,' he said, touching her cheek with his fingers in a chaste good night. 'But I'll be here, right on your doorstep. I don't want you waiting at the other end of the street.'

Macy found it hard to concentrate on her work the following morning. There was no question of her not getting anything done but each time she looked at her drawing board Brice Sinclair's face seemed to dance before her eyes. Then, to her surprise, inspiration started to flow, a lightning co-ordination springing up between her fingers and eyes with impressive results. After months, when she had thought she was no longer capable of producing anything beyond what was mediocre, really good patterns began to evolve, delighting her.

When she had first began working here, Macy's youthful enthusiasm, combined with her inborn talent for design, had produced results which George Paley had said might make her famous. After she had broken the rules and sold one of her designs to another firm, guilt had driven her to strive to improve her work continually and it had never made sense to Macy that exactly the opposite had happened. The harder she'd tried, the less satisfactory her work had become. Now, for the first time in months, she felt she was getting somewhere, and excitement made her cheeks glow.

Brice Sinclair might be indirectly responsible, she knew. During her lunch hour she pondered over this. Through the night she had decided it wouldn't be sensible to see Brice again but now she wondered if she dare give him up? If her work was going to benefit from his presence was she entitled to give him up? It might be a muddled way of thinking but anything that helped her work must help the firm and, goodness knows, she owed them enough!

Macy drank a cup of coffee without realising what she was doing. Who was using who? she wondered miserably. Brice wanted her but he didn't love her. She wanted him and she tried to pretend it was for the sake of the firm, while even to think of him sent the blood soaring through her veins. Having tasted his kisses there was an insatiable desire inside her for more. If she was going to be guilty of combining business with pleasure who was to know? She only knew she had to see him again and that none of the reasons, either for or against such a decision, seemed to matter.

Thelma had the day off so Macy didn't see her until the next morning. During coffee break, she paused by Macy's table. All Macy's spare moments were filled with thinking of Brice and such thoughts were all the company she desired. She was acting like a love-sick teenager but she couldn't help it.

She glanced up reluctantly when Thelma sat down in the chair opposite. 'Mind if I join you?' Thelma smiled.

As she already had, there didn't seem much point in her asking but Macy said politely, 'Please do.' She was never quite sure how far she could go with Thelma, even when she was in a good mood.

'I just wondered how your date went?' Thelma sugared her coffee twice and looked at Macy enquiringly.

'My—date?'

'Oh, come off it!' Thelma exclaimed. 'You know who I mean! That gorgeous Adonis who knocked you down then picked you up.'

Macy flushed. 'You do have a nice tactful way of putting things,' she said dryly.

'Well?' said Thelma belligerently.

Macy sighed. 'I don't think he'd appreciate being called an Adonis, and we only had a quiet meal.'

'Sounds about as exciting as a wet night at the seaside,' Thelma muttered disparagingly. 'Knowing you, that must just about sum it up. I don't suppose you even got as far as first names?'

Macy could see Thelma was fast losing interest and felt relieved. 'I did my best,' she murmured meekly.

'Of course you did,' Thelma's smile was both pitying and patronising. 'The trouble with you is you're far too slow. You'll have to change your ways, I'm afraid, if you're ever to have a successful relationship.'

Macy wondered what Thelma meant by that, while she hoped the other girl wouldn't ask if she was going to see Brice again. She wouldn't lie to Thelma but she had no wish to hear any more of her good advice. Thelma considered she was an authority on men. She was certainly popular with them. She always said she was only waiting for the right one to come along before she got married.

Thelma, fortunately, had things on her mind which concerned her more than Macy's date with a stranger. She hesitated then announced importantly, 'The new owner's here, had you heard?'

'No,' Macy glanced up blankly. 'I only heard he was coming.'

'He's been here a few days, well, on and off, actually.' Thelma took out a compact and viewed her smooth face complacently. 'It's rumoured he's quite a man— and I'm going to meet him!'

'Good for you,' Macy had no intention of annoying Thelma by seeming surprised. 'When?'

'Well, actually,' Thelma confessed, 'it was George who was supposed to be meeting him, but as he's away, I'm to go instead of him. In this case,' she smiled mysteriously, 'I'm going to make sure his loss is my gain.'

Thelma returned from the meeting of the heads of the departments with their new boss, looking even more triumphant than when she'd set out. It was late afternoon when she paused beside Macy's desk. 'For once rumour got it right,' she smiled, as Macy looked at her enquiringly. 'He's a dish and I like him.'

'But did he like you?' Macy teased, scarcely recognising Thelma in such good spirits.

'He certainly stared at me hard enough,' Thelma replied with great satisfaction. 'I can always tell when a man's interested and boy, is he something!'

Macy hid a small grimace of distaste. 'Does he seem a reasonable kind of man?' she asked, more interested in his policies than his appearance. 'Do you think he will make many changes?'

'Changes?' Thelma was still dreaming. 'Changes? Oh, you mean, Mr Sinclair? A few, I think. He's certainly very different from his uncle.'

'Mr—Sinclair?' Macy licked suddenly dry lips.

Thelma nodded. 'He's the new owner.'

'Mr Pearson was his uncle?'

'Well . . .' Thelma shrugged, 'Someone thought old man Pearson was his uncle but someone else didn't think the relationship was that close. I expect we'll find out in time but it's not that important.'

Sinclair! The name was wheeling painfully through Macy's head. It couldn't be! It must be coincidence, surely? 'Rings a bell, does it?' She recalled the mockery in Brice's voice as he had asked the question. Still she found it difficult to believe he wouldn't have said something if he had been the Mr Sinclair who now owned Pearsons.

Her own voice echoed back as she remembered the rest of that conversation. 'I don't want to know . . .'

She had refused to listen so how could she blame Brice if he had omitted to say who he really was? He had obviously been ready to tell her about himself but she had been so emphatic about not wanting to know.

And, yet, he had been very secretive when they first met, hadn't he?

'When he was so friendly,' she heard Thelma continuing thoughtfully, 'I was going to give him a hint that I was free, this evening, but I heard him refusing Bob Slater's invitation to dinner. Said he had already made arrangements, so I decided to wait. Wonder where he's going?'

If Brice did own the factory. No, Macy rephrased that sentence as a preoccupied Thelma wandered off and left her. If the Brice Sinclair she knew was the same man who owned the factory then she wouldn't see him again. While she argued with herself that he couldn't be, a mocking voice whispered that it was no use evading the truth. Despairingly she dropped her head in her hands, smothering a low groan. How could she have so foolishly fallen for a man who, if her suspicions proved correct, could never be for her?

As Macy lifted her head, Thelma turned at the end of the department, the small secretive smile on her mouth giving easy clues as to where her thoughts lay. Pausing only for a moment to check the time, Macy grabbed her coat and escaped before Thelma could come back to her. Her car had been ready that morning. She had asked the man who delivered it to let her have the account but he'd told her it had already been settled by Mr Sinclair. Macy had been dismayed and vowed to repay Brice whatever the sum he had handed over this evening. Now, she could only feel disgusted with herself that the ease with which he threw his money around hadn't made her suspect anything. If he did own factories, as well as heaven knows what else, how he must be laughing at her!

Miss Kirby had agreed to stay again. She had said, when Macy had asked her, that it was just as easy as going home to a cold house, especially when Macy would be there to take over from her later. What Kate needed was a night nurse as well as a day one but Macy knew she couldn't afford it. She was thankful that she was young, with the strength to endure broken nights so she could be there when Kate called for her.

She was wearing a new outfit when she ran out to meet Brice that evening. On impulse she had purchased it in her lunch hour but if Thelma had mentioned the name of their new boss earlier she doubted if she would have bought it. Her new outfit consisted of a pair of fine black velvet trousers and a black chiffon top with silver polka dots. It was something equally suitable for both formal and informal occasions and somehow she looked fabulous in it. With Brice in mind, she hadn't been able to resist it though she had hesitated anxiously over the cost. She sighed now as she realised she might not be with Brice long enough for him to appreciate it and her lovely new clothes might be doomed to spend the rest of their lives hanging uselessly in her wardrobe.

Brice was waiting as she left the house at exactly eight o'clock. As she slipped in beside him, he glanced at her soberly as he adjusted her seat belt but didn't speak. Words seemed somehow unnecessary and she made no attempt to break the silence between them as he sped off down the street. He seemed cool and remote yet a sudden hot gleam of desire was back in his eyes as he turned his head at the first set of traffic lights and murmured softly, 'I hoped I hadn't dreamt you.'

'What made you think you had?' Macy asked, her pulse reacting swiftly to the light pressure of his hand.

'I don't know.' His hard mouth twisted wryly as they moved off again. 'It was just a feeling I've had that you couldn't be real. You'll have to promise me you won't disappear and leave me?'

She frowned uneasily. 'What makes you think I might?'

'Again, intuition.'

Macy glanced at him quickly. If he was who she thought he was, she would be disappearing, at least from his immediate vicinity. If what she suspected was true she wouldn't be going out with him again. Nor would he wish to take her anywhere if he knew what she had done! Swallowing hard, she chided herself for not asking him outright who he was. Yet, somehow, when it came to it, she couldn't find the courage. Instead, she heard herself asking weakly, 'Where are we going?'

'Don't you recognise landmarks?' he teased.

She gazed rather blindly through the windscreen. 'Where you took me before?'

'Right first time,' he smiled.

Nervously Macy unclenched her hands, trying to get rid of the tension gripping her. The hotel where he had taken her before was very high class and popular. She wasn't sure why she wished they had been dining elsewhere unless it was that she wanted nothing to spoil her memories of that first, near perfect evening. Whatever the outcome of this evening, she felt certain it wouldn't be nearly as pleasant.

Furtively she glanced at Brice's forceful profile as he negotiated the oncoming traffic to reach the car park. The other night he might have told her voluntarily all about himself but he might object to being questioned. The hardness of his face, even in repose, was a clear indication that his position in life—whatever it was, had not been achieved through softness. There was enough power and temper beneath that controlled surface to make far braver persons than herself shiver. So far she had only known his kindness but she still remembered his anger at the factory gates when she'd nearly crashed into him. She had no wish to see it again, for if he was ever really furious with her, she doubted that she would ever survive it.

If her misgivings about the hotel didn't decrease, she did her best to hide them. But inside, when Brice drew her towards the lifts instead of one of the restaurants, and told her that they were dining in his private suite, she couldn't suppress another flare of anxiety.

CAPTIVE OF FATE 51

Being a man who missed very little, he saw it immediately. 'Macy!' he exclaimed impatiently, 'I don't intend leaping on you the moment we're alone. I've had a busy two days and I need to relax, that's all. If you really object I can easily get a table in the restaurant.'

'No!' Macy shook her head, doing a little quick rethinking. If Brice and she were to quarrel over what she must ask him, she would rather it happened where no one could overhear. Voices were very easily raised in agitation and she had no wish to attract that kind of attention.

Another couple joined them and as the lift rose there was no further chance to say anything but Brice appeared to take her acquiescence for granted. His suite was on the first floor. As he opened the door and ushered her through it, she asked mechanically, 'Do you like living in hotels?'

'I'm only here until some other accommodation is ready,' he replied briefly as the door closed behind them.

Macy wasn't a girl to be overly impressed by her surroundings but she felt her eyes widen as she glanced round the room she was in. It was furnished like a lounge with a dining area set discreetly through an archway in the wall at one end of it. Everything she could see smacked of top-class quality. Macy's knowledgeable eye noted how the curtains were made of the same exclusive material that covered the large three piece suite. Across the acres of deep carpeting half open doors led to what were obviously bedrooms although the glimpse of a desk in one suggested Brice might be using it as a make-shift study. Her heart sank as she realised he must be a very wealthy man to be able to afford a place like this, however temporary!

She turned, she wasn't sure whether to congratulate or accuse him but he was so close that she collided with him, with an impact that robbed her of breath. Something leapt in his eyes as his hands came out to steady her and he drew her swiftly into his arms, as if he was both hungry and thirsty for the feel of her—to have her close to him.

'It's been two whole days,' he said huskily.

Macy's heart began pounding as she felt his breath feathering her face and his body moving closer to hers. Indescribable surges of longing swept over her which she was almost powerless to resist. Desperately she fought against it. She had things to clear up before she could even allow him to touch her, yet here she was, in danger of forgetting everything but the feeling rising swiftly between them.

As she sighed raggedly his breathing roughened and her own became suddenly erratic. 'Macy!' he groaned, his lips moving across her neck before descending on her mouth, whatever else he had been going to say was cut off as their burning mouths came together.

Blindly Macy clung to him, returning his unconcealed passion. Who he was no longer seemed to matter. All that was important was that they were here like this. Her fingers dug convulsively into his shoulders and she heard his murmur of pleasure as she felt his warm skin through the thin material of his shirt.

'Macy,' he eased away from her slightly, putting a brake on their emotions as they threatened to flare out of control. 'These last two days have been the longest I've ever passed. I longed to be with you. If my business hadn't been important I would never have left you.'

Macy froze into a statue under the look he gave her. She heard him draw a long shuddering breath as he studied her flushed face and darkened eyes. All her fears returned but when she tried to push him away he wouldn't allow it.

Drawing her back to him, his arms tightened. 'Kiss me, my sweet,' he commanded softly. 'Don't fight it. You know as well as I do that it's what we both want.' Lowering his head, he added thickly, 'Forget everything but the two of us.'

Fiercely he gathered her to him, parting her quivering lips with his demanding mouth. Macy's arms crept round his neck and her senses vibrated in wild response as his hand slid under her jacket and blouse to find the warm curve of her breast. All sense of reality slipped away as she felt a violent stirring deep inside her as her awakening desires began surging in answer to his.

He had picked her up when a knock on the door interrupted them. His glance returning ruefully from the direction of the bedrooms, he put her gently down again but made no attempt to hide the hard excitement in his eyes.

'We'll have to wait,' he groaned. 'This must be our dinner.'

Leaving her, he went to the door while Macy did her best to calm her racing pulses. It didn't seem possible that she could be reduced to such a state in so short a time. While Brice was holding her, kissing her, her only thought had been to get even closer to him. If he had taken her to his bedroom she couldn't have fought him for the hypnotic effect he had on her made it impossible for her to resist him.

Self-disgust washed over her, leaving her feeling sick as she watched Brice organising the arrival of their meal. How could she have allowed her feelings to get so out of control when she still didn't know if Brice was the man who now owned Pearsons? Even if he wasn't, she despised herself for giving him the impression that she was the kind of girl who thought nothing of jumping into bed with a man she had just met. She hadn't been slow to recognise the derisive triumph in his eyes as he had picked her up before their dinner arrived, and she knew if she had let Brice make love to her she might have been filled forever with self-contempt.

Feeling the heat in her cheeks, Macy turned her head, hoping no one would notice. The waiters, fortunately, weren't curious, or if they were, they pretended not to be as they served the meal and departed with a minimum of fuss.

Brice had helped Macy off with her coat, now he shrugged out of the jacket of the dark suit he was wearing. 'Do you mind?' he smiled. 'It gets rather warm in here.'

Macy shook her head and attempted to concentrate on what she was eating. Through the thinness of his shirt, the rough hair on his chest was darkly visible but she tried to ignore how much it disturbed her.

He didn't seem any hungrier than she was. 'I suppose we'd better try and eat something,' he muttered, as if there were other things he'd rather be doing.

'This soup's very nice,' Macy made a determined effort to return to normality. Brice was too experienced, he was going too fast for her, and she was suddenly frightened of the emotions he was able to arouse in her.

She saw his eyes wandering over her slender young figure, taking in the way chiffon and velvet clung provocatively to the swell of her hips and breasts as she sat down. With his eyes on her, she was glad she had something new to wear, if she still wasn't too happy over the money she had spent.

'New is it?' he asked, brows raised enquiringly.

'Yes.' She wasn't aware that she was crumbling a roll into tiny pieces.

'For my benefit?'

Helplessly she nodded. 'I bought it today.'

'It suits you.' His eyes teased softly. 'But you would look beautiful wearing nothing, Macy.'

Feeling the hot colour run up her neck, she hated him, for she was sure that statement was nowhere near as innocent as he made it seem. 'I'm glad you approve,' she murmured stiltedly.

'Oh, I approve all right—of everything I've seen so far.' The warmth of his voice implied he would have no fault to find with the rest.

As Macy's colour deepened, he leant nearer and took

hold of her hand. 'I have to have room to eat!' she protested nervously.

He removed himself a few inches. 'Make the most of it,' he growled. 'It could be some time before you eat again.'

Again there were implications in his voice that disturbed her although she managed to shrug and smile coolly, as if she was well used to this kind of sophisticated repartee and it didn't bother her.

While Brice busied himself lifting a bottle of wine from the ice-bucket and popping the cork before pouring it out, she stole a glance at him sideways. She hadn't noticed before that he was so powerfully built, without his jacket his shoulders were massive. Her eyes dropped to where his trousers encased strong muscular thighs then quickly returned to where his dark hair was dusted with silver at the temples. At this juncture something seemed to hit Macy, leaving her pale and shaken.

Brice placed a glass in front of her and raised his own. 'To us,' he said.

Macy felt forced to drink with him but he didn't notice her silence nor the way her fingers curled tightly round the stem of her glass.

'What have you been doing with yourself since I last saw you?' he asked softly, gazing deep into her eyes.

'Just the usual things.' She avoided his searching glance.

He frowned, as if he was suddenly seeing something about her for the first time. A hand came out to tilt her chin towards him and his eyes narrowed. 'For a girl of your age, Macy, you're looking much too tired. You're either working hard or you've something on your mind?'

Aghast she stared back at him. Her tiredness came from too many broken nights with Kate but the something on her mind was guilt and she had very nearly forgotten about it. She felt ashamed that she had come here tonight to discover if what she had done need affect her relationship with Brice then allowed herself to be side-tracked. She suspected she had been unconsciously, if not deliberately putting it off and it must stop.

'Macy!' She heard Brice asking urgently, 'What is it?'

Her cheeks white, she answered him numbly. 'I've been hearing things today.'

'What kind of things?' he demanded tersely, as she hesitated awkwardly.

Oh, God, she bowed her silky head, never anticipating it would be so difficult. 'Thelma Brown,' she whispered, 'who's deputy head of my department, met the new owner of the factory today. She called him, Sinclair. Of course I knew it couldn't be you...'

Brice broke in grimly as he glanced at her sharply. 'It is me. I tried to tell you.'

Shock shook Macy as her head jerked up to stare at him. Helplessly she breathed, 'I never dreamed...'

Again he interrupted. 'How could you, but don't make it sound as if either of us had committed a crime. I didn't insist on your knowing, the other evening, when you refused to listen. You were clearly on edge and it wasn't immediately relevant. I thought it could wait but I did intend making sure you knew tonight. I didn't set out to deceive you. There wouldn't have been much point, not as far as I was concerned anyway.'

She tried twice before she was able to speak. 'But surely you can see it makes a difference?'

'Why should it?' he countered patiently. 'Being the owner of Pearsons doesn't make me a different person. I'm still the same man as I was before.'

Miserably Macy looked from his impassive face to the sole in wine sauce now congealing on her plate. What she had learnt about Brice might not have been so alarming if she'd had nothing to hide herself. He hadn't done anything wrong—she had! When she thought he had nothing to do with the factory, she had

CAPTIVE OF FATE 57

been tempted to accept his company as a means of forgetting what she had done. Now she knew she never could. Brice was her new boss, and while Mr Pearson might have been lenient when the moment of confession came, she knew instinctively that Brice would be an entirely different proposition.

'I just think it would be better if we didn't see each other again,' she whispered bleakly.

'Give me one good reason?' he snapped.

'Maybe I can't,' she replied tautly, 'but I still think it would be best.'

He ate a mouthful of fish which he seemed to enjoy like sawdust. 'Macy.' He eyed her steadily while laying down his fork. 'You and I are going to continue seeing each other, whether you like it or not, but first we have to talk.'

'What about?' she gulped, wondering how she might manage to make him change his mind without immediately betraying her miserable secret? If it hadn't been for Kate she would have told him, there and then, and taken the consequences, but for Kate's sake she needed her job, at least until it no longer mattered.

He paused, his mouth tightening. 'If you aren't hungry,' he said, 'let's go back to the lounge. We can always get some sandwiches later.'

Unhappily Macy stumbled to her feet. She would rather have gone home but she realised he wouldn't let her. When they were seated on the wide sofa in the softly lit lounge he insisted she had some brandy with her coffee and though she felt she didn't want any, she had to admit that it steadied her. She was glad he made no attempt to touch her though.

He waited until she finished her coffee then turned to her, his eyes a great deal cooler than she had seen them. 'Now,' he said grimly, 'I'm going to tell you a few things which I hope will make you realise just how foolish you're being. First I'm going to start with Alec Pearson. He was my mother's cousin and although I had met him a few times I had no idea he was going to leave me anything.'

'You got everything!' Macy wasn't conscious of the faint awe in her voice.

Brice's hard mouth twisted. 'Everything,' he observed dryly. 'And, as you're interested, everything comprises of several run-down, heavily mortgaged factories, scattered throughout the country. All of them a liability.'

'How can you say that?' Macy's own troubles were swamped by quick indignation. 'Why, the one I work in, here in Manchester, must employ hundreds of men and women.'

'It's the only one that could be making money if it was properly run,' he shrugged. 'The others will have to go.'

'Can you do that?' she gazed at him doubtfully. 'I mean, just close places down?'

Grimly he shook his head. 'No. You have unions to make sure nothing's that easy. Every close-down has to be negotiated every inch of the way. It means a lot of work.'

Macy frowned suddenly. 'You talk as if you didn't belong here?'

He smiled faintly. 'You're very discerning. I've lived for years in the States. My father ran a similar business to Pearsons there and I took over from him.'

Looking at him, Macy flinched, her huge blue eyes dominating her face as her colour ebbed again. She felt both relieved and unhappy—if it was possible to feel both emotions at the same time. 'Then you won't be staying in England . . .?' she said slowly.

CHAPTER FOUR

BRICE returned Macy's uncertain glance steadily. 'I intend staying for a while, anyway. Sometimes I feel my roots are here, call it the pull of warp and weft or what you will. Another thing, Alec Pearson honoured me by bequeathing me his life's work, such as it is. When people trust you to that extent you can't let them down.'

Macy flinched as this hit at her own conscience. Brice was a hard man but clearly one with principles. 'Won't you miss America?' she asked.

'Yes,' his eyes lingered on her face, 'but there are compensations and the prospect of restoring a run-down business is always a challenge.'

A little colour returned to her cheeks. 'Is the business very run down?'

He smiled sympathetically as he caught her thread of anxiety. 'I don't envisage a loss of jobs in the Manchester works. In fact, after I've had a proper look at what's been going on and dealt with the culprits, we may need more staff.'

'Culprits?'

'I was speaking theoretically, not of people. Once the rot sets in, in anything, it's difficult to stop. Too many opportunities have been missed, especially regarding sales and promotion. We can't just sit at home waiting for the orders to come in, we've got to go out and get them. I've just scratched the surface so far but I can guarantee from now on there will be changes beneficial to the firm.'

Brice spoke so confidently it wasn't difficult to recognise his enthusiasm and drive. In other circumstances Macy would have admired it but now it only made her shiver.

'So you see, my sweet,' his voice softened as he gently took hold of her hand, 'there's no need to fear for your livelihood. I'm no ogre, as you'll find out if you please me.'

'I—I'll do my best.'

'I hope to see a lot of you, Macy.'

Her blue eyes lifted anxiously to his face, her lips suddenly dry with apprehension. 'But you'll be busy.'

'To begin with, yes,' he agreed ruefully. 'In the States I rarely let up but I'm never going to devote twenty-four hours a day to any business again. We'll have the evenings and weekends, Macy. You can also lunch with me.'

His grey eyes were alight and gleaming. Macy didn't know how to answer him. If she refused to see him again he would simply take her in his arms and make nonsense of all her protests. It might be better if she could somehow cause a natural rift between them so that he wouldn't suspect she had done more than change her mind about him? Even the most determined lover must be repelled if he received no encouragement. Not that Brice was her lover yet, she reminded herself hastily, but if she could put an end to the growing friendship between them before it had a chance to deepen into a more meaningful relationship then he wouldn't be able to accuse her, when the dreadful day of her confession came, of having led him on in the hope of receiving his forgiveness!

'I'd give a lot to be able to read your thoughts,' Brice mocked gently.

Her long lashes dropped in confusion. 'You have to make sure they're worth it.'

'Now,' he teased, 'you're insulting. I believe you were thinking of me?'

'Yes.' She couldn't help smiling and her blue eyes danced as she looked at him again. Brice had a sense of humour, she liked him in a mood like this, even if he was a little too sharp for her.

'Anything else you'd like to know?'

She shook her head. 'I suppose there is but you've told me a lot already.'

'Let's keep the rest for another time,' he suggested wickedly, tightening his hold of her hand to draw her closer. 'You can ask me all you like over lunch, tomorrow, but we can do more than talk here.'

Aware how her colour flowed hotly, Macy clenched her free hand against her hip. 'It's getting late, Brice.' She was surprised to see it was after ten. 'I must go.'

His tolerant expression fled. 'You aren't a child, surely, who has to be home by a certain time?'

The harshness of his voice sent a cold feeling through her rapidly beating heart. 'My aunt's ill,' she began almost parrot-fashion when, as if to punish her, he pulled her roughly into his arms.

'Your aunt can't always be ill,' he snapped. 'You've only been here a couple of hours which we've wasted talking. You can spare me a few more minutes.'

Macy sensed the tension in him nearly matching her own as he bent his head forcefully. Trying to evade his swooping mouth was a futile exercise. Desire flooded her as Brice crushed her lips under his and strained her trembling body to him. When she began clinging to him it was the invitation he had apparently been waiting for. With a grunt of triumph he parted her burning lips to allow entry for his exploring tongue. While she gasped and squirmed and clung even harder, his hands slipped under her blouse to cup the rounded contours of her breasts, touching off a new wave of sensuality. She shuddered in growing excitement as he nuzzled her slender neck, the sensitive hollow of her throat then the creamy skin below until she thought she was going crazy.

Outside, someone dropped what sounded like a tray of glasses in the corridor, the noise loud enough to bring Macy to her senses. 'Please, Brice,' she breathed, 'let me go.'

His face was hard and faintly flushed. He glanced furiously towards the door then gave in. 'Hell!' he muttered, 'I'm paying enough for peace and privacy.'

He rose reluctantly, drawing her up beside him, but when she turned her back on him to tidy her clothes he pulled her derisively against him, letting her feel the hardness of his unsatisfied body. His hands covered her breasts, holding her tightly while he pressed a savage kiss on her bare nape.

'Until tomorrow,' he promised thickly.

She was still trembling as they went downstairs. Her feelings for Brice were getting out of control. She had to do something, for her own sake and his! The situation was bordering on dangerous.

Brice placed a possessive hand on her waist to guide her from the lift and he didn't remove it. Crossing the foyer, Macy was so strung up that she didn't see Thelma until she bumped into them.

Thelma started to apologise then stopped. 'Macy!' she exclaimed, her eyes widening. 'Fancy meeting you here.'

Macy blinked, a feeling of disaster already upon her. She wondered if Thelma had stopped in front of them deliberately but her surprise seemed totally genuine. 'Hello,' she murmured stupidly.

Thelma wasn't wasting her attention on Macy. She was staring at Brice and the arm he had round her as if she couldn't believe what she was seeing. 'Mr Sinclair,' she gasped.

Brice inclined his dark head, a faint smile on his mouth. 'Miss Brown.'

Thelma was with two other people who moved politely out of earshot. Macy, becoming aware of the unfriendly glances Thelma was darting at her, felt puzzled. She was with Brice but was this any reason for Thelma to make her feel she was committing a crime?

'I had no idea you and Macy knew each other,' Thelma was exclaiming effusively to Brice.

She was clearly curious and he didn't enlighten her. His smile merely altered enigmatically as he steered Macy adroitly past her. 'Macy and I are just leaving,' he said smoothly. 'I expect we'll meet again, Miss Brown.'

The next morning Macy hadn't been at work five minutes before Thelma pounced on her. 'Well!' she demanded contentiously, 'what was all that about?'

After the first quick glance, Macy kept her eyes focused on her drawing board. She knew what Thelma meant and despised herself for attempting to avoid the issue. 'What was what all about?'

'You and Brice Sinclair!' Thelma hissed, incensed.

The loudness of her voice caused Macy to glance round in alarm, to make sure no one was listening. 'He's the man I nearly had a collision with.'

'Nearly!' Thelma sneered sarcastically.

'I never tried to deceive you,' Macy replied. She disliked feeling forced to offer an explanation. Was it any of Thelma's business? Why did Macy always feel it was necessary to keep on the right side of her? 'I had no idea that the Mr Sinclair who rescued me was the same Mr Sinclair who'd inherited the factory. I couldn't confirm it until last night.'

Thelma appeared to digest this slowly. 'So you won't be seeing him again?'

Macy swallowed. 'Actually I'm having lunch with him.'

'Lunch! Today?' As Macy nodded, Thelma stared sharply at her pink cheeks. 'Why?'

Macy wasn't sure herself. 'He asked me . . .' she said helplessly.

Thelma looked on the verge of jealous rage. 'Are you sure you know what you're doing, Macy? You aren't in his league and you must know it. You ought to hear the stories about him and the American society girls he takes out. I shouldn't like to see you get hurt.'

Was Thelma aware of the hurt she inflicted herself?

Macy's soft mouth twisted wryly. Thelma meant well—usually. She was a good artist. Her designs were the bold, often savage kind that appealed to certain leading couturiers. She was dedicated too. The department meant a lot to her. Naturally she didn't want Macy involved in an affair that might upset her work.

Fortunately Thelma was called away, relieving Macy of the necessity of finding an answer. The morning passed quickly. Macy was grateful that she could lose herself in her work which was a great help when her worries became almost too much for her. She wished spring would hurry up, then she could seek fresh inspiration on the moors and in the valleys surrounding the city where the sight of a few clumps of primroses or violets, nestling against a sheltered bank, could fill her with new enthusiasm. Once she had thought of going to Switzerland to see the wild flowers there but Kate's illness and the money she owed the factory had caused her to shelve such plans indefinitely.

She was on late lunch. At one Brice came to the department for her. He strolled in as though he owned the place, which of course he did, Macy reminded herself unhappily as she reached for her coat. Seeing him talking to Thelma, she wished he had waited outside, as he had said he would. When Macy approached, Brice put an arm round her and Thelma smiled, masking her venom.

Macy could have sunk through the floor when Brice dropped a firm kiss on her cheek, his glance lingering with amusement as she blushed scarlet. 'I'm going to steal Miss Gordon for a couple of hours, Miss Brown,' he said, sweeping Macy from the room.

Macy was panting when they reached his car but more from agitation than being out of condition. 'You shouldn't have come to collect me,' she protested jerkily. 'It will only cause gossip.'

He frowned, his grey eyes cooling. She could see he was quite oblivious to the curious glances following them. 'Don't tell me what I can do, Macy,' he very nearly snapped. 'When I want something I go right after it. It won't harm you to remember.'

In the car he gave her another hard kiss but this time on her lips. Immediately it seemed as if high voltage electricity leapt between them. As he drew back she was startled to notice a shudder running through him and the knuckles of the hand he grasped the steering wheel with were white.

'See what you do to me?' he quipped, but the smile that twisted his mouth didn't reach his eyes as he steered through the factory gates and shot off down the street.

They lunched in a hotel on the outskirts of the city. It wasn't quite as large as the one where Brice was staying but it was just as luxurious. Macy wondered how he knew his way about so well. For a stranger he was remarkably knowledgeable on the best places to eat and how to get there. Again, as in the hotel where he stayed, his commanding presence appeared to rate top-quality service. They were ushered to what was clearly one of the best tables and waited on hand and foot.

Throughout the meal, Brice rarely took his eyes off her and made no apology for staring. Sometimes the grey eyes flickered with grim humour as if he couldn't believe what was happening to him. Macy cast nervous looks at him, at the strange restless uncertainty in his face, and trembled at the cruel line of his lips. Occasionally his body seemed rigid with tension and she feared it for it so easily aroused a similar response in herself. Her slim hands clenched on her fork and knife as she struggled to eat, feeling she was being consumed by desires demanding release.

Impatiently Brice pushed his barely touched plate aside. 'It's you I want, Macy, not this.'

His voice was so harsh she had to tease or lose her composure completely. 'Food will help you get the factory back on its feet better than I would.'

He sighed but picked up his fork again, a sardonic grin easing the stiffness round his mouth. 'Don't underestimate yourself, Macy. With people like you working for me how can I help but succeed?'

With people like her ... Macy's throat went tight. Too many people like her and Brice would soon be out of business!

When she paled, he exclaimed. 'What is it, Macy? Aren't you feeling well?'

She saw the smile wiped from his face as his eyes darkened with anxiety. Feeling guilty for the alarm she was causing, she murmured unevenly, 'I think I could do with some air.'

Immediately he called for the bill. 'Too stuffy in here.'

It wasn't but she was glad to leave. All the time they were together she knew a mounting desire to throw herself in his arms and the whole object of this lunch had been to put a little distance between them. In this she had failed dismally. So far as that went, the meal had been farcical. Every glance they had exchanged had been full of a craving to be closer to each other than convention allowed in public places.

Driving to a secluded spot, Brice ruthlessly demonstrated how fed-up he was of keeping his distance. Within seconds, Macy was lost in the circle of his arms as he covered her face with passionate kisses.

Impatiently he tore the ribbon from her thick, silky hair, breathing hard as he ran his fingers through it. Thrusting a hand under her jumper, he cupped her breasts then pulled her across to him to let her feel how aroused he was as he explored the depth of her mouth devastatingly.

'Darling,' he groaned. 'Let's take the afternoon off. We can go somewhere where we can be alone.'

'No.' It took a nearly physical effort to get the word out when every nerve in her body was urging her to agree. Colour flamed in her cheeks, making breathing difficult. 'I can't, Brice!'

Masculine violence leapt at her from hot grey eyes. 'I can't last out much longer, Macy.'

It chilled her that she felt the same way. 'We've only known each other a week,' she protested.

'Do you think I'm going to feel any differently about you in a year?' he demanded curtly.

'You probably will.' She thought that sounded sensible.

Brice stiffened, clamping her head in his hands, kissing her deeply. 'I've never felt before like I do when I'm with you.' He turned up her face, searching her pale features. 'You're beautiful, Macy, young and innocent, but that's only part of it. You realise what's between us makes it imperative that we belong to each other sometime? I'm ready to admit how I feel yet you're always holding back.'

She dare not agree for she couldn't tell him why. She thrust her guilt aside thinking bitterly that she was getting good at it. 'Nothing's very easy just now,' she murmured evasively. 'You have to give me time.'

His sigh was the epitome of frustration. 'I'm trying to.'

As if her fingers were rewarding him for patience, they crept to his face, feeling hard tension in jawbone and cheek. She massaged gently. It was a dangerous experiment and she held her breath. He had a tough face under the dynamic good looks. His features might have been carved from teak. She shuddered as he turned his mouth to kiss the racing pulse in her wrist. His easy sensuality spoke of expertise. How many other women had he caressed like this?

'I—I won't go to bed with you,' she stammered tremulously.

The grey eyes flashed with anger as he wrenched her hands off him. 'You're holding out better than most.'

She tried to understand the reason behind such vindictiveness but the hurt was there all the same. 'Am I?' she said sharply.

He went pale with remorse. 'Oh, God, darling,' he groaned. 'You've got me so I don't know what I'm saying.'

'I have to make sure you don't get the wrong idea about me,' she explained with some difficulty. 'I don't want you to think...'

'We get on better when we don't,' he interrupted dryly.

Macy giggled involuntarily. Brice's anger had disappeared and she loved him when he was like this, if she didn't read too much into what he was saying. She would have liked to have told him that she longed to stay with him forever. Too many things stood in the way of such a confession, however, not the least of them Thelma. It would be adding fuel to the fire of her temper to be late back from lunch.

She stole a glance at Brice from under her lashes. His face was becoming dearly familiar and he could rouse her to ecstasy without even trying. Thelma must think what she liked! Macy knew she couldn't insist on returning to the factory straight away. Why it should seem doubly important to spend some time with Brice, she wasn't sure. She only knew she had to.

'This Saturday,' he said, drawing her closer, 'we'll go walking. You can show me the Lancashire countryside. Do you like walking, Macy?' When she nodded he laughed with delight, 'I knew you would. It will be fun...'

'And cold,' she grimaced.

'If you get cold I'll soon warm you up,' he promised, eyes gleaming. 'I'll take you to my place for a hot shower when we get back. Would you like that?'

Shyly she smiled at him, her eyes dreamy. He was unashamedly lulling her, persuading her, making her powerless to resist. Her hands lifted to seek access through the front of his shirt and he immediately obliged by undoing the buttons for her. The skin underneath was crisped by dark hairs that stung her fingertips. As a gasp escaped her she sought to withdraw but a large hand clamped over both hers, holding her immobile.

'Macy!' he growled, kissing her so thoroughly her fingers curled convulsively in his. Releasing her hands, he sought her breasts, pushing her jumper aside to fondle their fullness. Her silky bra didn't cover much but he dealt with it swiftly. Then his mouth joined his hands, leaving a trail of burning kisses across her bare flesh. Macy unconsciously arched her back, pressing against him, unknowingly inciting him by her provocative movements. Brice muttered her name harshly as he caught a hardened nipple between his teeth, his passion now fully aroused.

'Brice,' she moaned as their burning mouths came together again as if they could never get enough of each other. Brice rolled over, never taking his demanding lips from hers as he covered her with the hardness of his body, crushing her fiercely down on to the seat.

Suddenly he drew back, letting her go abruptly. The air seemed to be dragging from tortured lungs as he buried his face in the arms he clamped round the top of the steering wheel. 'Not in a car,' he groaned, as if talking to himself. 'Not here, not like this!'

Macy groped automatically to tidy her clothing, her fingers all thumbs. Her heart was beating so hard she thought at any minute it might leap from her body and like Brice she was having difficulty with her breathing.

'It can't go on,' she heard Brice saying, his voice steadying and stronger although he didn't look at her as he started the car. 'We have to work something out, this evening, Macy, and whatever it is I don't expect to receive no for an answer. We're adults, not a couple of kids.'

Back at work, Macy hoped unhappily that she didn't look as disturbed as she felt. Thelma glanced at her then turned her head. When she looked again, Macy was relieved to see she was mistaken about the other girl's anger. Thelma eyes might be taunting but she was smiling.

'You don't usually return from lunch looking so dishevelled,' she teased. 'You'd better go and do something about it before the others begin noticing.'

Macy flushed crimson and realising this could only add to her general air of abandonment, she hurried to do as she was told.

Thelma followed her to the cloakroom, walking in while Macy was busy combing her hair. 'Are you seeing him again tonight?' she asked idly.

Macy's cheeks had no time to cool. 'I think so,' she replied warily.

Thelma washed some paint off her hands and the glance she cast at Macy over her shoulder was both anxious and kindly. 'Go carefully, Macy, won't you? At the risk of repeating myself, I shouldn't like to see you hurt. Charming men are a menace it takes experience to cope with. It's not always easy to say no.'

She wandered out again and Macy sighed with relief. When she had gone out with Brice she had thought Thelma might be jealous but clearly she wasn't. She was concerned for one of her team, that was all. Maybe she had a right to be, Macy conceded. After Brice's lunch-time kisses it would be difficult to settle down to work.

Being determined to forget about him for a few hours, she was dismayed when he came to see her later in the afternoon. She saw him speaking to George Paley then he came over and drew her outside.

'What is it?' she asked, wondering why every time she saw him every pulse in her body seemed to gather pace. He was the last person she had expected to see and she hoped he didn't intend making a habit of calling in at her department as frequently as this.

Brice stared at her in silence for a moment before he spoke, his grey eyes meeting hers intently. 'I can't make it this evening, Macy. There's a delegation coming from the Bradford works that I have to meet. The appointment was made by my secretary while I was in London and unfortunately she forgot to mention it until half an hour ago.'

The grimness of his mouth suggested that his secretary's oversight hadn't gone unrewarded. Macy felt sorry for her. 'Do you have the same woman who used to work for Mr Pearson?' she asked. When he nodded she pleaded, 'Don't be too hard on her, Brice. It's common knowledge that Mr Pearson's death was a shock and she's not so young any more.'

'I'm running a business, Macy, not a home for old ladies.'

A certain hardness in his voice made Macy uneasy and seeing it he relented. 'Miss Drake is due to retire in a few months' time on an excellent pension plus what Alec left her. I'm the one to be pitied, Macy, having to look for a new secretary. You don't fancy the job?'

'I'm not that clever or brave,' she grinned. 'I happen to be an artist.'

'You'd be clever enough,' he retorted mockingly. 'You've managed to keep me at a distance long enough.'

'It's not been that long,' she said nervously, not liking the glint in his grey eyes.

'I know!' His arm shot out to pull her to him with a repentant smile. 'It's only been days but it seems like an age.' His hand smoothed her hair at her temples as he kissed her briefly. 'I'm sorry about tonight, my sweet. If the meeting hadn't been so important I would have cancelled it. I don't even know what time I'll be through. These things have a habit of dragging on.'

'Perhaps it's just as well you're going to be busy, this evening,' she assured him. 'I might have found it difficult to get out.'

He kissed her again before he left. Fortunately the corridor was still empty. 'See you tomorrow,' he said, putting her from him reluctantly.

Macy dressed carefully the next morning in a blue

skirt and blouse, tying her hair at her nape with a matching ribbon. She felt she couldn't lunch with Brice every day in the jeans she wore continually. In jeans and smocks she had almost forgotten how fine-boned and slender she was. Her legs were long and beautifully shaped. Kate had teased, as she'd left, that it was a shame to hide them.

Yet despite feeling that she looked her best, all the way to work Macy's stomach played up. What was the use of pretending she could continue lunching with Brice, basking in his approbation? Today she must tell him what she had done. If she simply refused to see him again, he wouldn't listen, and she had no wish to concoct excuses he wouldn't believe. Even to think of his reactions made a sickness rise in her throat. Somehow she must convince him that she had sold the design for her aunt's sake...

Thelma was already there when she walked into the department. Thelma frequently arrived late. George Paley was always threatening not to forgive her and the mornings weren't exactly cheered by the sight of her sulky face. This morning something must have happened to please her for she was smiling.

She was still smiling an hour later when Brice's secretary rang requesting Macy to report to Mr Sinclair's office immediately. When Thelma gave her the message she said softly. 'Don't worry about hurrying back love. We're not all that busy.'

Macy was too preoccupied wondering why Brice had sent for her so urgently to take much notice. Usually Thelma grumbled at the slightest interruption in routine. Maybe he just wanted to see her? He might be as hungry for a glimpse of her as she was for him? Her spirits lifted then sank as she remembered that, no matter what he wanted to see her about, she had a confession to make. This might prove an ideal opportunity.

His office door was closed but Miss Drake, still

CAPTIVE OF FATE 73

enthroned in her usual domain, told her to go straight through. Macy hadn't been here before although she had spoken to Alec Pearson often when he had come to her department. He had taken a keen interest in her work and praised it on more than one occasion.

There was a short passage between Miss Drake's office and the one Brice was in. Macy opened his door after knocking briefly for Miss Drake said he was expecting her. In spite of reminding herself that the friendship between them must end, she smiled at him involuntarily when he looked up as she entered.

He was sitting behind his desk and other than glancing at her, he made no attempt to greet her. Macy's smile faded as she became aware of the harsh expression on his face. She clasped her hands behind her back to stop them shaking as she was struck by a premonition of disaster.

'What is it?' she whispered, forgetting to say good morning, forgetting everything but that it had to be something dreadful to make him look at her this way!

'Come in, Macy,' he said coldly.

Was he annoyed because she hadn't waited for his permission to do so after she'd knocked? It didn't seem so for when she began apologising he stopped her sharply and told her to sit down.

Her few words of remorse froze on her tongue as she groped her way to the chair opposite him. 'Is something the matter?' she persisted, now convinced that something was.

'Yes,' he replied shortly. 'There is. I received a letter this morning which has given me quite a shock.'

'A letter?'

Brice nodded. 'I don't know who sent it, they didn't sign their name but I find the contents difficult to believe.'

He made no attempt to keep the ice from his voice and coldness seemed to ripple through his large body.

Macy stared at him apprehensively. She had no idea what he was talking about but she had never seen him as grim as this.

'Won't you explain?' she pleaded.

'I think you're the one who's going to have to do that,' he said tightly. 'This correspondence concerns you and it's pretty damning ... As I've just said, it's unsigned but it has a strange ring of truth about it.'

Suddenly Macy knew what was written on the sheet of paper he picked up with a savage flick of his fingers from his desk. 'The writer states,' Brice rapped, before she could speak, 'that you sold one of your designs to another company while you were working for us.'

Macy's eyes were huge and stricken and a feeling of faintness came over her. 'You've found out?' she whispered hoarsely, both her attitude and words proclaiming her guilt.

'Then it's true!' Fury turned his grey eyes to a glittering silver, making her shrink in alarm. 'My God, Macy,' he rasped, 'I find it difficult to credit you would do such a thing. Well,' he snarled as she gazed at him mutely, 'have you nothing to say for yourself?'

'I—I was going to tell you,' she replied unsteadily, 'I intend paying the money back. I realise I broke the rules but I was desperate.'

His anger in no way abated. 'You receive a good enough salary. What was the money for? Clothes—like the outfit you were wearing the other evening?'

How could she make him believe that was the first thing she'd bought since Kate took ill? 'It was for my aunt,' she said haltingly. 'She was in hospital and wanted to come home but we couldn't afford it. She has to have constant nursing, you see. I got a thousand pounds, which was half the prize money for the design. It pays for Miss Kirby—she's the nurse, and other things. Kate can do very little for herself.'

Brice's mouth curled derisively at the corners. 'That I will need to see before I'm convinced you aren't lying.'

He paused, his eyes piercing her, 'Did you say it was only a thousand?'

'I put the money in the bank,' she hastened to assure him. 'You can check if you like.'

Glaring at her, he snapped. 'You aren't giving me permission to do anything, Macy. This will be investigated thoroughly with your permission or not.' He ran a hand through his hair, his expression stony with contempt. 'Didn't you know, when you broke the rules of your contract that the penalty could be severe?'

A red haze of weakness passed in front of Macy's eyes as Brice revealed what he intended to do. 'I was going to see Mr Pearson about it,' she said dully. 'After—after Kate didn't need me any more.'

Brice ignored this. 'You said it was half the prize money?' he suddenly exclaimed. 'The person who bought your design wanted it for a competition?'

'Yes,' she faltered, 'he did.'

His voice cracked with fresh anger. 'So—it was a man. Is he your lover?'

She whitened then colour blazed in her cheeks. 'How can you say that!' she choked. 'I never met him.'

Brice's fury subsided a little. 'All the same,' he said curtly, 'you'd better tell me his name?'

If she told him that it might betray Thelma. Confused she looked at him, unable to think straight. Apprehension was making her ill, numbing her mind. 'I can't,' she murmured starkly.

'You could go to prison,' he threatened cruelly.

'I'll tell you the name of the factory . . .' she offered desperately, proceeding to do so half-hysterically, without waiting to see if he wanted it or not. Kate would never get over it if she went to prison! 'I meant to pay it back,' she reiterated, trembling, 'but it was only three months ago, I haven't had a chance.'

The angle of Brice's jaw didn't soften any but he stopped asking questions and appeared deep in thought. During the few moments' silence which followed he gave no clues as to what he was thinking but his demeanour was such that Macy knew she was far from being forgiven. She sat shaking, not daring to speak, fighting against unhappiness and terror until she feared she was going insane.

Eventually he took a bunch of keys from his pocket and tossed them to her. 'Go and wait in my car,' he muttered abruptly. 'I have a call to make which may take some time but I'll join you as quickly as I can.'

'But my work?' she protested anxiously. 'Mr Paley will be wondering where I am.'

'You aren't returning there until this has been cleared up,' he said grimly. 'Now leave me and stop asking questions.'

When he joined her and they shot out of the yard there was no visible change in his appearance. When she asked, in some trepidation, where they were going he told her to wait and see. It wasn't until minutes later that she realised he was taking her home.

CHAPTER FIVE

As they sped past familiar landmarks, Macy gasped. 'Why can't I go home by myself? I'll have to go back for my car.'

'You can collect it in the morning,' Brice said impassively. 'I'm taking you home, as I told you, so I can see for myself how ill your aunt is, before you have a chance to hatch something up. Your previous reluctance to introduce me to her has done little to convince me that your story regarding her is true.'

Macy stared at him in a state of continuing numbness. Her whole world had collapsed. Brice was a stranger, no longer the man who had wanted her passionately. Now every glance he spared her was an assurance that he wanted nothing more to do with her. She felt frightened and ill but he had no sympathy. Not that she deserved any, she admitted dully, but if he had cared for her even a little, wouldn't he have at least tried to understand why she had been driven to act as she had done?

Outside the house where she lived, he stopped so abruptly she was jerked forward. Within seconds, without a word of apology, he had hauled her from the car to the front door. Thinking of Kate, Macy's spinning senses steadied protectively. 'You won't tell my aunt anything?' she begged, her face ghastly pale. 'She has no idea where the money I received really came from. I told her I'd had a rise in salary.'

'Take me to her,' he commanded curtly, promising nothing, withholding even this small grain of comfort.

Miss Kirby met them in the hall, surprised to find Macy home at this hour. 'Is something wrong, dear?' she asked anxiously, looking curiously at Brice's grim face.

'Nothing's wrong,' Brice replied smoothly, before Macy could intervene. 'Macy has the rest of the day off and wishes me to meet her aunt.'

Miss Kirby frowned uncertainly as Macy introduced her. 'Your aunt isn't so good this morning, dear, but if you don't stay too long it should be all right. I know she's been hoping to meet Mr Sinclair.'

'Just a few minutes,' Brice promised and, as Macy hesitated, his fingers dug into her arm.

Impotently Macy led him to the dining-room which had been converted to a bedroom when Kate could no longer manage the stairs. Woodenly she said, 'Come this way.'

Kate Gordon was barely able to get out of bed. Daily her condition worsened. She grew weaker and the drugs she was obliged to take in order to keep her suffering to a minimum made her frequently too drowsy to be fully aware of her surroundings.

She opened her eyes when Macy appeared though and her smile reflected the courage which allowed her to triumph over her physical disability. 'Macy?' she murmured. 'You're home early.'

Macy nodded. 'I've brought someone to see you, Aunt Kate.'

Brice leant nearer, grasping the inert white fingers. 'Miss Gordon,' he smiled. 'I'm Brice Sinclair.'

Macy was glad his eyes were warm rather than compassionate. Kate hated pity.

'My niece has talked a lot about you,' she said slowly. 'I knew Alec Pearson. At one time we were good friends.'

Brice squeezed her hand gently, his glance flickering over the room before returning to Kate's emaciated figure.

'Macy's very good to me,' the sick woman sighed. 'I don't know what I should have done without her. She has her own life to lead though. That's why I was so pleased when you—persuaded her to go out with you.'

Brice touched her hand again and said he must go but that he would be back. As he ushered Macy out, Miss Kirby came in to attend to her patient and Macy invited him into the lounge.

'You told your aunt who I am?' he commented dryly, when they were alone.

'As soon as I knew myself,' she said nervously.

'Boasting about me, were you?' he scoffed. 'There's always some fool ready to fall for a scheming little traitor like yourself.'

'I wasn't boasting,' Macy swallowed. 'And I don't scheme. If the design business hadn't happened so quickly, I don't think I'd have gone through with it. I wish I hadn't!' she said bitterly.

Brice stared at her, his grey eyes darkening. Taking a step towards her, he stopped, thrusting his hands deep in his trouser pockets. 'It's obvious you weren't lying about your aunt,' he said tersely. 'Maybe we can work something out. Meanwhile, I'll see you tomorrow. Report to my office at eleven o'clock.'

He turned away but she clutched his arm, her eyes tormented. 'Do I still have a job, Brice? I need one desperately, and if you don't want me . . .'

'I still want you,' the coldness of his voice made her shiver. He didn't allow her to mistake his meaning—which wasn't hers. 'As for what you're going to do—shouldn't you have thought of that sooner?'

'I was going to repay every penny!' She wondered if he would ever believe her.

'Don't tell me that again,' he snapped, ripping his hands from his pockets to push her aside impatiently. Striding to the door, he spoke over his shoulder. 'I'll send someone to fetch you in the morning. See that you're ready.'

Macy had never felt so miserable in her life. She was worried, too, the tension inside her almost unbearable. It took a superhuman effort to pretend everything was normal, so as not to worry Kate. Her aunt, however, was more curious over Brice than as to why Macy had the day off. Macy spent a lot of time evading questions she had no wish to answer. She wouldn't be going out with Brice again but she had no desire to arouse even more curiosity by confessing this to Kate.

Shock from the morning's disclosures was still sweeping over her in waves. She couldn't forget the contempt in Brice's icy grey eyes. She had been falling in love with him. Even if he forgave her would anything ever be the same? What was the use of protesting her innocence when she had committed a crime and was definitely guilty? In Brice's shoes, she doubted if she would have reacted differently. The evidence against her was conclusive, to say the least, and he clearly wasn't prepared to listen to a plea of extenuating circumstances.

Wearily she puzzled over the letter he had received. Only Thelma could have written it. Her brother would have risked too much and had nothing to gain by betraying her. Yet what had Thelma to gain? Macy frowned as the answer seemed all too obvious. Thelma had taken a fancy to Brice and was jealous because she believed Macy was trying to steal something she wanted. There was a chance, Macy pondered, that she could be wrong, but not knowing for certain was going to make working with the other girl almost impossible.

Macy was ten minutes early at the factory next morning. She had been waiting outside when the car Brice sent had arrived. As she sat in Miss Drake's office, waiting for him to summons her, she wondered if he was already arranging for her arrest? Her hands were clammy with sweat while the rest of her was cold with apprehension long before he buzzed Miss Drake with orders to send Miss Gordon in.

He was standing beside his desk and glanced at her briefly as she opened his door and closed it behind her. She felt so nervous she could see little at first. His face was a blur until she blinked and focused properly.

CAPTIVE OF FATE

'Good morning,' she faltered, not able to think of another thing to say to this cold-eyed stranger facing her.

'Good morning,' he returned curtly, 'Sit down.'

At least he didn't bawl her out. He was being polite. The tension of oncoming tears gathered in Macy's throat as she obeyed. She supposed she should be thankful for small mercies, even if they might be likened to the wine a prisoner was sometimes offered before execution!

Sitting with her hands tightly clasped in her lap, she wished he would put her out of her misery. At last, when she could stand his prolonged and contemptuous surveillance no longer, she whispered beseechingly, 'Brice . . .? What have you been finding out? What are you going to do with me?'

'One question at a time, I think,' he said grimly, ignoring a tear on her cheek. 'The evidence against you is quite conclusive, I'm afraid.'

'I realise that,' Macy swallowed convulsively. 'If you would wait until Kate has gone before you prosecute . . .'

Brice Sinclair's mouth tightened. 'There has to be something but it might not come to that. There's an alternative that I might put to you.'

As she looked at him blankly, he went on coldly. 'It may seem a bit of a coincidence but when you mentioned the name of the firm you'd sold your design to, I remembered I'd had dealings, in the States, with the man who runs it. Unfortunately, yesterday, when I managed to locate his place of business, he was away. I spoke to him this morning though.'

After a pause, during which Macy waited in frozen silence, Brice shrugged. 'He informed me that his company has gone into liquidation. In other words, he's bankrupt. Well, after expressing the usual regrets, I asked him if he had any good artists in their design department going spare, but he said the best ones had already been snapped up. One Oliver Brown, whose work had won a regional award, this year, had gone abroad. He believed to South Africa. So,' Brice's voice lashed savagely, 'it didn't take a lot of intelligence to connect the Mr Brown who'd worked for him with the Miss Brown who works for me and to hazard a fairly accurate guess as to what was going on. Am I not right, Macy?'

Miserably she nodded. She was past trying to be devious. He apparently knew it all, being so expert at working things out. What was the use of trying to oppose him, she would only be fighting a losing battle

'Thelma Brown wrote that letter.'

Yesterday he had asked and she had refused to tell him. Today he stated it as a fact with absolute confidence. Nervously she murmured, 'There's no proof...'

'Macy!' he rasped. 'For God's sake use your brains! Can you think of anyone else? Do you want me to refresh your memory by spelling everything out? Are you going to make it easier for both of us by telling me voluntarily what happened, or do I have to force it out of you?'

Unhappily she looked at him, swallowing a sob. 'You seem to know most of it already but I'll tell you,' she agreed. 'Thelma knew I was worried about Kate. She was also worried about her brother being made redundant but she believed if he did well in a competition that was coming up, he would be kept on.'

Grimly, Brice interrupted. 'And Mr Brown needed fresh inspiration. He probably never used your design, Macy. At least, not in its original form. More likely he combined it with a few ideas of his own. People like that are too crafty to put themselves at risk so easily.'

Most of this was beyond Macy. Brice was much more knowledgeable about this kind of thing than she was and what Thelma's brother was doing—or had done, didn't seem as important as the trouble she was in.

CAPTIVE OF FATE

'Why should Thelma betray me?' she asked bleakly. 'She must have known you might trace who wrote that letter, even if you have no actual proof?'

'I don't know why she should wish to betray you. She probably believed that you would be dismissed after I'd sent for you and you confessed and that it would go no further. Maybe she is aware that her brother's firm has closed down, so whatever she did couldn't harm him. But she definitely used the information to harm you.'

Macy winced bitterly. It was all a nightmare! What had happened was something she would regret all her life yet only one thing seemed immediately important. 'Have you forgiven me?' she whispered.

'Forgiven you!' If Macy had put a match to dry tinder the flames couldn't have moved faster. He was beside her in a flash, fury lending brute strength to the arms which lifted her bodily from her seat. As the breath was knocked out of her by the suddenness with which she was imprisoned against him, he said harshly, 'When are you going to realise what you have done? Not only have you broken the contract you signed when you joined the firm, that design you sold could have cost us much more than the thousand you received for it. If one of our customers had seen it and been impressed by it, they might have left us in minutes. Business is as fickle as that today. No one can afford to take chances. Yet, here you are, indignant that someone's had the audacity to betray you when you were so ready to play traitor yourself. And you talk of forgiveness!'

'You've got it all wrong,' she sobbed, as his tongue lashed her. 'I know I deserve the poor opinion you have of me but I didn't mean to harm anyone. I only did it for Kate and I thought I could pay the money back. I didn't realise what it could involve.'

'Didn't you?' His voice was insolent and no warmer.

'If you'd give me another chance?' she pleaded, trying to stem the tears she could see were annoying rather than appeasing him. She didn't want him to think she was deliberately attempting to gain his sympathy.

'Give you another chance?' Rage, it seemed, was causing him to repeat things after her. 'Do you take me for a fool? Do you seriously think I'm going to sit here waiting for you to sell something each time you get short of money?' His grey eyes glittered into her dilating blue ones, with the hand gripping the front of her blouse threatening to choke her. 'By rights your case should go before the board. If it wasn't that I wouldn't wish to see anyone so beautiful serving a prison sentence, I wouldn't hesitate. But whatever happens, I'll never trust you again.'

As his voice and eyes cut her to ribbons, Macy wrenched away from him. She felt sick and ill but all she could think of was Kate. For her sake she forced herself to grovel. 'I have to work, Brice,' she begged, her pride in shreds. 'Kate and I couldn't manage without what I bring in.'

As she backed from him until she hit one of the office walls, he followed to imprison her once more with his arms. 'Go home and sack the nurse, my sweet,' he advised, the dryness of his voice making a mockery of his words of endearment. 'Send the nurse away and look after your aunt yourself. With your devious little brain I'm sure you'll soon find another man to help you.'

'That's no use,' she began.

'Well you're no use here,' he snarled, clamping her chin with an iron hand to make her look at him. 'Don't try me too far,' he warned, 'I'll never let you near the design centre again and I'll find a way of making sure you don't sabotage anyone else, even if it kills me.'

The coldness of the smile he bent on her was nothing to the cruelty of the mouth that descended to crush her lips. Macy felt herself growing faint as the electric feelings that shot through her mingled with the heartache she was already experiencing. Her breath caught as the office whirled but when she tried to escape him again his arms tightened. Brice was kissing her as if he was trying to assuage both anger and disappointment, then he thrust her away from him, breathing hard.

'Go home, Miss Gordon,' he said roughly, as Macy drew air into her tortured lungs. 'I'll be in touch in a day or two.'

Instead of going home, Macy began looking for work. She wasn't in a fit state to start trying to find work immediately but she felt it was imperative. Neither Kate or Miss Kirby knew anything was wrong so they wouldn't be expecting her back before her usual time. Unfortunately she had no luck. Personnel at the job centres were naturally puzzled that she appeared to have left a firm like Pearsons simply because she felt like a change.

Brice didn't come until the evening of the third day. Miss Kirby had gone, it was after eight and Kate was sleeping when Macy answered the door. She was startled to see him and the nervous reaction in her stomach whitened her already pale face. Since he had almost thrown her out of his office, for all he had said he would be in touch, she hadn't expected to see him again. That he was here could only mean one thing, that he intended to conduct her punishment personally. Otherwise wouldn't he have communicated through his solicitor? Dully resigned, Macy stared at him. She couldn't expect to get off scot-free. She had committed a crime and must pay for it.

'Invite me in,' Brice Sinclair's mouth tightened as he observed the unconscious terror in Macy's eyes. 'I'm no ghost, even if I'm about as welcome.'

Blindly she headed for the lounge but he stopped her. Catching her arm he drawled, 'What's wrong with the kitchen? It must be warmer.'

'It's a—a bit untidy,' she stammered.

He pushed her in and closed the door.

'I have to listen for Kate,' she protested, feeling trapped.

'I've sharp ears,' he grunted, glancing indifferently round the small room. The table was covered with scraps of paper. Too late, Macy remembered the figures she had been trying to tot up.

Brice pounced, his trained eye reading the sorry state of her finances immediately. 'You aren't going to be solvent long,' he remarked unsympathetically.

'It's none of your business!' Trying to inject some righteous indignation into her voice, she failed dismally. Gathering the scattered sheets together, she realised she was wasting her time.

'What have you been doing since we last met?' he wondered glibly, sitting down on one of the hard kitchen chairs without waiting to be asked and loosening the buttons of his jacket.

Had he reminded her of their last meeting deliberately? Hastily she averted her starved eyes from the breadth of his chest. 'Looking for work,' she replied briefly.

He merely smiled.

Feeling like hitting him, she turned to switch the kettle on. She didn't want anything herself, nor did she want Brice to think she was trying to keep him here, but it was something to do. She couldn't bear to just stand gazing at him.

'We've only instant, will that do?' she asked flatly.

Absently he nodded. 'You don't sound as though your job-hunting forays have met with success?'

Resentfully she glanced at him as she spooned coffee in two cups. Brice wouldn't know the meaning of failure. She had tasted it these past three days and found it bitter. 'Without proper references or a reasonable reason for leaving the factory, it isn't going to be easy.'

'Do you expect anything to be easy, after what you've done?'

'No.'

'Then stop whining.'

Suddenly Macy's control gave out. Flying to him, she dropped down beside him, anguished eyes fixed fearfully on his unrelenting face. 'What are you going to do about me, Brice? Have you changed your mind about prosecuting?'

'It wouldn't do much good,' he said harshly.

She swallowed but felt no great relief. 'There's Thelma,' she whispered. 'She knows what I did and she must have had a reason for telling you about it. Will she be satisfied if nothing dreadful happens to me?'

Brice's grey eyes frosted. 'Miss Brown would probably have been satisfied if I'd dismissed you and had nothing to do with you again. I don't believe she's that vindictive but she's gone. She's left Manchester for good to join her brother.'

Macy was stunned. Her blue eyes widened incredulously. 'How did you persuade her?'

'Never mind,' he said curtly, and, as Macy frowned, 'I can assure you no violence was used. We came to an arrangement that suited us both. She got off much lighter than most people do when resorting to blackmail.'

'Blackmail?'

'There are various kinds.'

Macy felt at loss, not knowing what to make of what Brice was telling her. She couldn't imagine Thelma going meekly or even staying away. She had been looking forward to taking over the department once George Paley retired.

'Will she be able to settle in South Africa?'

'It can probably be arranged,' He met her eyes mockingly. 'Don't look so anxious, Macy. I'm sure it's not usual for one criminal to worry over another. S.A. is still a good place to live and I'd be willing to bet that Miss Brown is going to take full advantage of all it has to offer. She had thought of joining her brother anyway, but whatever happens we won't be seeing her here again.'

Macy drew a sharp breath. 'You soon get rid of people, don't you?'

'If I get rid of people,' he drawled, 'it's in the pleasantest possible way. I never do anything that's outside the law.'

His voice gave nothing away. He sounded indifferent but Macy sensed she wouldn't be wise to drive him too far. Her brief flash of defiance faded and she bit her bottom lip uncertainly. 'That only leaves me ...'

'It does,' he agreed coldly, 'It hasn't been easy deciding what to do with you.'

'I'd like to return to the factory,' she said impulsively. 'I suppose it wouldn't be any use asking you to give me another chance?'

'It wouldn't,' he snapped. 'I don't trust you.'

'You've told me that before.'

His eyes narrowed as he replied chillingly. 'I couldn't let you return, Macy, without reporting what you have done.'

That alone would ensure her second dismissal, he didn't have to spell it out. 'But, if no one knows?' she argued desperately.

'Hell!' he said, losing patience. 'Don't you understand? Even without taking you back there's enough complications. In not conferring with the board, I have to take full responsibility. I can't run the risk of the same thing happening again, should another firm employ you. They would immediately come back to me and I'd have to take the consequences.'

She was dismayed by both his words and his tight, furious tone. And horrified that he had so little faith in her. 'It won't happen again,' she said dully.

'The only way I can ensure that it doesn't is by marrying you.'

Macy could only stare up at him in silence, shocked to the marrow, totally dismayed. 'W—what did you say?'

'You heard,' he retorted grimly. 'We're going to be married.'

'No!' she jumped to her feet, her soft mouth working, 'That's impossible.'

Grimly he shrugged. 'It's all I can think of.'

His indifference hurt so much she nearly screamed. Her cheeks were faintly flushed, tears drenched her blue eyes making her swallow painfully. Looking at him, she faltered, 'You don't love me . . .'

'I don't,' he agreed. 'Can you wonder?'

The mockery in his voice seared her, causing her to flinch. Wearily she shook her head. 'No, but it's a fact.'

'Love isn't necessary for the kind of marriage we will have,' he said.

Macy shivered beneath his contemptuous glance. He was tall and broad, essentially, utterly masculine, yet she remembered his tenderness when he had made love to her. Now, although she took full blame for his changed attitude towards her, she would never have believed he could be so dispassionate. In other circumstances she would have been overjoyed to marry him, caring for him as she did. In other circumstances, she told herself bitterly, he would never have asked her!

'What will you be getting out of it?' she asked tonelessly.

'I'll make sure it's enough,' he taunted, his eyes lowering meaningly over her trembling figure.

It dismayed Macy how all her pulses leapt in response. She wanted nothing to do with him yet her body constantly betrayed her. The unnatural pink in her cheeks deepened as her hands clenched tightly. 'It wouldn't be possible for me to marry anyone,' she said dully. 'I can't leave my aunt and she wouldn't leave here.'

'She wouldn't have to,' he said smoothly. 'I will take over from the moment we're married. I'll supplement Miss Kirby with a night nurse and domestic help. Your aunt won't want for a thing.'

'She would never accept.'

'I think she is past the stage when independence is important any more. Your happiness would come first.'

Macy gazed at him in helpless bewilderment. He had an answer for everything. It would delight Kate to believe Macy's future was secure and she was becoming daily less aware of what was going on about her.

'What's the alternative?' Brice interrupted her thoughts softly. 'With the best will in the world, I can't let you return to the factory. And,' his voice hardened, 'this is the only way I can keep an eye on you. You won't be getting such a bad deal either. You'll be atoning for your sins in complete comfort and security. Gossip has a way of getting around and hurting people but, as my wife, you'll be able to ignore it.'

She couldn't allow herself to be so easily persuaded! 'I'll find some kind of work,' she said desperately. 'I don't care what I do.'

He laughed mirthlessly. 'No kind of jobs are easy to find, Macy, especially in areas of high unemployment. And you have your aunt to think of as well as yourself.'

'I don't know what to say!' she choked, too bitterly conscious of the truth of his remarks.

'Yes will do.'

She started to protest but her voice cracked, forcing her to pause and consider. 'It appears I have no choice,' she said at last.

'Not exactly the most flattering form of acceptance,' he mocked. 'You'll have to see, in future, that your responses are more to my liking.'

'I don't think either of us is in this for pleasure,' she gasped, as he rose suddenly and yanked her up beside him, into his arms. 'You only want revenge!'

'Maybe,' he snapped. 'Why not?'

She had spoken at random. Revenge hadn't occurred to her before. Now she wondered—revenge for what? He gave her no time to dwell on it though. Jerking her closer, his mouth descended on hers before she had a chance to evade him.

Brice showed her no mercy and his ruthless kisses seemed to supply the answer she had been seeking. Like in the office, the other day, he was punishing her for what she had done, and in consequence ruining a friendship from which he had expected to derive more pleasure than from the marriage he was contemplating.

Realising this, she again tried to fight him but felt her head whirl as familiar stirrings began anew. She trembled violently as he strained her against him until she felt she must break. It seemed incredible that her arms should be determined to struggle round his neck while he continued to bruise her mouth with savage kisses which actually hurt her.

'Please stop!' she moaned as he freed her mouth for a second.

'Revenge is going to be very sweet,' he mocked. 'If that's what I'm after.'

'You're hurting me,' she gasped. 'How can you be so callous?'

'It's coming easily and you deserve it,' he retorted, but his next kiss wasn't so painful.

Nevertheless, she broke away from him, not knowing whether his cruelty or the tenderness he briefly displayed was the most difficult to withstand.

'Had enough?' he taunted.

She had to concentrate on other things or she might have said no. Unhappily she bent her head so he wouldn't see her hot cheeks. 'Where will we be living, Brice? Unless you're prepared to wait, I couldn't leave Manchester for a while yet.'

He respected her reluctance to say because of Kate but shook his head emphatically over waiting. 'We'll be married right away, Macy, and living here. Alec left me his house along with everything else. I've been hesitating about going to live in it on my own but things are different now.'

She would rather live in a house than a hotel, even an apartment. 'As long as it's not too far away,' she said hesitantly. 'I would like to be able to visit Kate as often as possible.'

'You can visit every day,' he promised. 'Just as long as you're home every night.' When Macy blushed as his voice lowered huskily, he added. 'I'll take you to see the house at the weekend.'

True to his word, Brice came for her on Saturday, after lunch. Macy's eagerness to see her future home had been replaced by an odd reluctance but, because she couldn't explain it, she said nothing. By this time she had resigned herself to marriage with Brice. Any love in their union would be on her side but she hoped eventually he would come to love her as much as she did him. He must care for her a little or he wouldn't have asked her to marry him? When he kissed her she could feel something running through his hard body. If he'd felt nothing for her, would he have insisted on seeing her again after they first met? As he already knew many beautiful women, it couldn't merely be sex.

Reassured by the faint hope which her deliberations encouraged, she smiled at him tentatively when he picked her up. He didn't appear to notice her smile and she tried not to let it matter. If she was going to feel hurt each time he ignored her she mightn't survive very long. Composed, she commented how lucky they were that the sun was shining.

Brice disregarded this too. 'I saw you in town this morning,' he said.

Macy glanced at him quickly. Was this why he was so grim? He wasn't looking at her. He was concentrating on getting along the street. Usually it was empty but at weekends there were children about. He spoke evenly but she sensed his disapproval.

'I had things to get for Kate which aren't stocked locally,' she explained.

'Did you see anyone you knew?'

So that was it. 'I didn't meet anyone from the firm, if that's what you mean?'

'I'd rather you avoided the people you worked with,' he replied coldly. 'You must have plenty other friends.'

'This past year I've dropped most of them.'

'Because of your aunt?'

Macy shrugged. 'There didn't seem much point in making dates when I wasn't free in the evenings. I found it easier to limit myself to those I knew at the factory.'

'You miss them?'

'Yes,' she confessed. 'Textile designing isn't the isolated career some people imagine it to be. I was part of a team, both in my studio and out. A good designer has to work very closely with the technicians and mechanics who run the machines. I spent a lot of time on the shop floor discussing dyeing processes.' She halted awkwardly, suddenly embarrassed, 'You shouldn't have let me ramble on,' she murmured. 'You know all this, of course.'

'I do,' he agreed, 'but that doesn't mean I'm tired of hearing it. Did you ever get to London or abroad?'

'Once,' she replied. 'George and Thelma usually visited the big stores and customers in London.'

'Did you never think what you might be giving up?' he asked curtly.

Seeing his mouth tighten in sudden anger, Macy sighed. She knew what he was hinting at. She would never have given up anything voluntarily but she had never been that career-minded. 'I could work freelance,' she suggested.

'No,' he forbade harshly.

That didn't seem reasonable. 'Why not?' she exclaimed.

Amazingly he seemed at loss for an answer, or it might have been that his attention was briefly diverted by having to pull up at a crossing. 'You're too good,' he snapped, when she thought he was going to ignore her. 'You'd have people clamouring for your designs and I can do without that kind of competition.'

'I just thought it would be something to keep me busy.'

'I'll find you something else,' he retorted, in such a tone that she couldn't tell if it was a threat or a promise.

For the remainder of the journey they travelled in silence. Brice's features were set and each time Macy glanced at him an icy shiver crawled down her spine. Despite his occasionally relaxed manner, it was obvious he hadn't even begun to think of forgiving her. It would take time, she realised, chiding herself for being too impatient. Rome wasn't built in a day! and it was no use indulging in self-pity. She had to look at things from his point of view. She had to give him time to learn to trust her again—she could only pray that for both their sakes, this wouldn't take too long.

CHAPTER SIX

BRICE had said the house was on the outskirts of the city and Macy had envisaged a pleasant situation with trees screening it from other houses in the immediate vicinity. Her heart sank as he turned off the main thoroughfare into a long, neglected looking road.

The houses on either side were large and detached but run down. Slates were missing from roofs and green damp encroached on walls. Gardens were overgrown with last year's dead leaves fluttering soggily on wet ground. The short drive Brice turned into was no better. Grass fought for supremacy with eroding tarmac, leaving barely room for a car to pass. The house they approached was as large as its neighbours and in the same shabby state. Macy gazed at it doubtfully.

Too late she realised she wasn't being very tactful when she observed wryly. 'This must once have been a fashionable district.'

Brice retorted sharply. 'Alec Pearson lived here so it should be good enough for you.'

Macy lowered her dark lashes blocking out the pain reflected in her blue eyes. 'I didn't mean . . .'

'Whatever you meant it makes no difference,' he cut in savagely as they walked to the front door. 'You'll be living here whether you approve of the district or not, so you'd better be prepared to make the most of it.'

'I'm sorry,' she whispered.

Glancing at her pale face, Brice appeared to experience a brief remorse. His tone softened slightly as he inserted a key into the rusty lock. 'I admit,' he confessed, 'before I met you, I was thinking of selling. It seemed too big for a man on his own but now that I'm going to have company, I'm sure it will prove ideal.'

Smothering her doubts, Macy followed him inside. It must be exactly as Alec Pearson had left it. There was plenty of space but it was dark and depressing and the atmosphere could scarcely be called inviting.

'The panelling's nice,' she commented, trailing after Brice and, to make up for her former remarks, trying to please him. 'With a little imagination and the right furnishings it could be made very attractive.'

'Spending my money already, are you?' he snapped. 'Can't you wait until we're married?'

Macy moved away unhappily. 'I wasn't . . .'

He swung her around to him roughly. 'Haven't you even the courage of your convictions?' he taunted. 'You have to stop retracting everything you say that doesn't please me. I have no respect for cheats but I have less for cowards.'

That stung and she gulped, stemming tears. 'At least I try to please you. You never try to please me!'

'Why should I?' he countered, grey eyes glittering. 'You're a thief and a liar. I'd be betraying everything decent in me if I considered you at all.'

Sensing a determination in him to override any plea she might offer in her own defence, Macy didn't antagonise him further by attempting to argue her innocence. Turning from his cold face, she wandered upstairs. Here the colour schemes were even more depressing than those on the ground floor and she shuddered to think of the effect they might eventually have on her. Such drabness would be continually at odds with her artistic nature.

At least it was all spotlessly clean. Everything was shining and it struck her as being slightly incongruous. Wouldn't cobwebs have been more appropriate in such surroundings? She sighed and tried to inject a little humour into her gloomy thoughts, but it wasn't easy. With the house so dark that she expected to be confronted by Alec Pearson's ghost around every corner, instead of feeling happier, she began to believe that everything was against her.

When Brice found her and it was obvious that his depression was greater than her own, she searched for something to take the grim expression from his face. 'Everything's very clean,' she smiled tentatively.

'I had a cleaning firm in,' he replied. 'They will come each week, once we're married.'

Macy stifled another sigh. She would have liked to have managed herself but she sensed Brice was waiting, with a cutting remark for her to protest. Then there was Kate, whom she must visit regularly. And meals? Brice would require breakfast and dinner, some days he might even be in for lunch. Which would all take time and on top of this there would be household shopping to do. If she ran out of jobs to keep her occupied there was always the garden. Almost eagerly she ran to the window to gaze down on it. It was large and overgrown but instead of dismay she felt a thrill of anticipation. If she had time to spare she could tackle that! It might be difficult to envisage flowers growing in such a wilderness but she could make a start.

Turning back to Brice, she was startled to find him standing right behind her and her heart began beating rapidly at his close proximity. 'I—I was looking at the garden,' she stammered breathlessly. 'Once I had a home with a garden and I enjoyed getting dirty in it. Of course I was only a child.'

'Indeed?' Far from impressed, Brice fixed aloof eyes on her flushed face. 'I'd have thought you'd be more interested in where you were going to sleep.'

'I am upstairs,' she murmured evasively.

'This is a guest bedroom.'

She had glanced into the master-bedroom but hadn't lingered. 'Where I sleep is up to you, I suppose.'

'I'm glad you realise.' Satisfaction edged his hard mouth as he noted her cheeks growing hotter. 'You appear to be learning.'

His tone was so arrogant that when he took her in his arms she tried to evade him. As his face darkened, she wondered despairingly how long it would take her to recognise his moods, and stop making mistakes that aroused his anger.

'I've told you not to fight me,' he said coldly, drawing her closer, speaking against her averted cheek. His tongue traced a path to the side of her neck, sending a thrill of awareness down through her body. She felt a surge of unsatisfied longing as his hands tormented the outer curves of her breasts and his mouth crushed hers in ever deepening hunger. Parting her lips with a sigh, she heard him groan.

It took every bit of will power she could find not to curve her arms about his neck. I mean nothing to him, she kept telling herself. He might want me but how much does he care? Once I belong to him will he want me again? Dear God, though, I love him! she moaned to herself.

'Macy?' he stirred slightly, his teeth nipping her lower lip as he sensed her inner resistance. That she shuddered in response to his sensuous cruelty didn't altogether satisfy him. As suddenly as he had taken hold of her, he thrust her away from him.

As she regained her balance and stared apprehensively, he grated, 'Don't ever hold out on me again, my sweet. Once we're married, I'm going to see that you abide by the rules of the contract you'll agree to and sign. And you can take that shocked expression off your face. There'll be no opportunity for breaking it this time.'

Their marriage contract, as Brice chose to call it, was duly signed, two weeks later. After the brief ceremony in Macy's local church, they returned to Kate's house for an hour. Miss Kirby had made the cake and sandwiches as a wedding present and Brice provided the wine. Macy had made small plates of savouries and a cream gateau early that morning. It all looked very nice set out on the table they had carried to Kate's bedroom so she could at least share part of the day with them.

CAPTIVE OF FATE 99

The minister proposed a brief toast and Brice replied to it. He surprised Macy by never leaving her side and she could see this pleased Kate. She told herself this was why he was being so attentive but couldn't deny herself the opportunity it afforded to pretend that theirs was a normal marriage and she was the usual happy bride.

She was wearing a creamy dress and jacket and with her thick hair knotted at the back of her head, she looked beautifully cool and elegant under a small hat composed of flowers and short veiling. She had held out firmly against a traditional wedding dress. It was because Kate had pleaded that she had dressed even as much as this. If she had followed her own inclinations, because of the kind of marriage she was making, she would never have bought anything new.

Brice made her doubly conscious that their marriage was a mockery when he muttered derisively as they were leaving the church. 'I suppose you aren't entitled to wear white.'

Macy didn't reply. Feeling both stunned and hurt, she couldn't bring herself to look at him. The gold wedding ring on her finger felt like a ball and chain and she experienced all the dread of a prisoner unable to escape.

In his car, which he was driving himself, Brice glanced at her white face and said tersely. 'None of this is easy for you, Macy, and I didn't help matters with that particular remark. It was actually meant as a question.' He paused, a pulse jerking in the tightness of his jaw. 'I've been wondering about you but I've no intention of judging you. I've been around myself.'

Stubbornly she hadn't satisfied his curiosity. Whether he condemned her for it or not, she knew he believed she'd had affairs with other men. She wasn't so naïve not to know that while few men expected their bride to be completely innocent, not many liked to think she had been willing to jump into bed with every man who had asked her. Perhaps, Macy thought bitterly, it might be a form of revenge she could indulge in herself, if she could even briefly withhold the truth from him?

'I'm going to miss you, dear,' her aunt whispered, with the first sign of breaking composure Macy had witnessed since her father died. 'Look after her, Brice, won't you?' she appealed to him, her voice strengthening with urgency. 'You don't know what a wonderful wife you're getting.'

Brice patted Kate's hand and said he realised how fortunate he was. 'I'm going to treasure her all my life,' he assured Kate firmly and only Macy seemed aware of the underlying threat. Her punishment was not going to be over quickly. There would be no release.

She was startled when he bent his head and kissed her but she guessed again that this was for the sake of her aunt. His mouth bruised down on hers and the kiss went on and on. Macy felt the world drift away as she suddenly clung to him.

Miss Kirby's delicate cough drew them apart but Brice went on looking at her. 'Goodbye, darling,' Macy whispered to Kate, 'I'll probably see you tomorrow.'

Farewells weren't drawn out for Kate was tired, but, even so, they had stayed longer than they'd intended. It was nearly dusk when they left to drive to the house which was to be a new home for both of them. They were not going away anywhere. For neither of them would it be practical. For Brice there was too much at stake at the works and Macy wouldn't have been happy far from Kate, whose tenuous hold on life could be broken any time.

The house in Valley Road looked exactly the same as when Macy had last seen it two weeks ago. The windows and doors had been repainted, she noticed, but it was too dark to see properly. Inside, Brice must have had the central heating seen to as well for the rooms were warm instead of cold and unwelcoming. Most of Macy's clothes were already here and she suddenly longed to get out of the dress she was wearing.

'It's been a long day,' she said haltingly, feeling Brice watching her again.

'And not over yet,' he said softly.

She felt her pulses beat faster and murmured quickly. 'I'd like to change.'

'You don't have to.' His grey eyes regarded her thoughtfully. 'We aren't going anywhere.'

What was he insinuating? Turning, she stumbled upstairs. She didn't wish to go anywhere. She hoped he didn't think she expected to be taken out for dinner. She had no inclination to go out again, this evening, yet she felt more weary than tired and oddly keyed up.

Clenching her hands to control her unconscious fears, she tried not to let her feet falter as she heard Brice following her. As he took her arm and guided her to the master bedroom, she was relieved in a way that she wasn't going to have to ask him where she was to sleep. Would he leave her here, she wondered, and go off and spend the night elsewhere? Despite his veiled threats, she realised he might. He might choose to play cat and mouse with her, waiting until her nerves were in shreds before making their marriage a proper one. Becoming aware of this, she didn't know whether to be glad or sorry.

In their room, she was surprised when he closed the door and the glance he bestowed on her scattered any rational thoughts. A warm flush stained her creamy throat at something she saw in his eyes. 'If you're hungry,' she said hastily, 'I can easily cook you something?'

'I'm hungry,' he confirmed, his mouth twisting, 'but it isn't for food, my sweet.'

She didn't pretend not to understand him but she found it difficult to believe that a man with his looks and experience, even if he had married her, could really want her. Staring into his dark, rugged features, she wondered why. I'm nowhere near attractive enough for him, she thought unhappily. What she couldn't see was the haunting beauty of her small, pale-skinned face and some quality in her slight, delicately boned body that aroused the urge to protect—and possess in men. She guessed something about her appealed to Brice but had no idea what it was.

Noticing tiny flames beginning to dance at the back of his glittering eyes, she turned away but he moved faster. Crossing the large room in a few long strides, he turned her around to look at him. Noticing her slightly defiant stance, he snapped, 'You aren't going to try and cheat me, are you, like you did Alec Pearson?'

His words sent a chill through Macy but also a thrill of something else. 'I've no intention of cheating you— of anything,' she cried. 'I was just going to get undressed.'

'Were you?' Clearly he was undecided about believing her. 'Then you'll need some help.'

He might have been throwing down a challenge a more sophisticated adversary would have understood but Macy wasn't sure how to reply. Was she ready for such intimacies yet? Controlling all but a faint tremor, she said, 'I can manage.'

'Why not pretend you can't?' Brice taunted. 'It's much more fun.'

Already his eyes were discarding her wedding finery but fear clogged her throat to an even greater extent as he began kissing her seductively. For a second she panicked and struggled to tear away from him. Constraining her easily, his free hand gripped her waist, turning her fully to him. Spreading his fingers, he moved his hand insiduously to the base of her spine, then, drawing her tightly against him, he let his other hand coil around her neck.

He was hurting her a little but in a new, exciting way against which she had no defence. It seemed she had a deep well of passion inside her that she had never been aware of before, which was responding to the demands his hardening body was making on hers. Suddenly she found herself clinging to him, melting within the circle of his arms.

When he eased away from her slightly, she felt bereft until he said, 'If you aren't hungry why don't we go to bed? Unless you want to go downstairs again?'

'No,' she gulped, 'I don't want to go downstairs.'

'And—bed?'

He wasn't making it easy for her. The colour in her cheeks deepened and she wasn't able to meet his mocking eyes. 'Yes,' she whispered.

He didn't renew his offer to undress her. As she stood trembling before him, he began doing it automatically and so expertly that she realised this couldn't be the first time he had applied himself to such a task. Licking dry lips, she felt glued to the spot but oddly acquiescent as he carefully removed every garment she wore. He worked slowly, as though it was a ritual he enjoyed and didn't intend to hurry.

Beginning with her jacket, he slid it gently from her shoulders, dropping it to the carpeted floor. When her zip came down, her dress joined it, falling in a whisper of chiffon while he paused to kiss the warm white skin of her shoulders. Then, as she vainly tried to slow her runaway heartbeats, he drew her silky slip over her head with a murmur of satisfaction, leaving her in only her bra and panties, which barely covered anything.

Grasping her narrow waist, he pressed his mouth first below then just above her lace and satin bra. 'Your heart's pounding like mad,' he said softly, as it raced wildly under his lips.

She shivered and her eyes closed as his lips brushed her forehead. 'It's because I'm not used to making love like this,' she whispered helplessly.

His lips widened in a smile but she couldn't see what kind it was. Possibly he didn't believe her but she had no wish to look at him and see only mockery in his expression. Wildfire streaked through her veins as her breasts tautened to his touch and she expected, any moment, to be disrobed of what little she had left.

She was so absorbed in concentrating on what he was about to do next that she gave a small start when he taunted softly in her ear, 'I'll leave you something to keep you feeling respectable while I get rid of my own things.'

Did he expect her to help him, as he had helped her? Anxiously her eyes flew open but as if he had read her thoughts he grinned again and shook his head. 'Tonight I'll do it myself, my sweet,' he laughed, 'You're trembling so badly you might never finish.'

Following words with actions, he discarded the expensively tailored suit he had worn to their wedding as though it was something he had picked up at a jumble sale. Because she was staring at the floor, rather than him, she saw it drop on top of her own clothes already scattered there.

Her breath coming softly, Macy was about to retreat in instinctive panic when he warned her to stay where she was. She obeyed but had to fight for composure before she could look at him. When she did, the faint smile she was dredging up vanished as her eyes encountered her husband's naked body. She gulped, colour leaping frantically to the surface of her skin as she stared dazedly, unable to comprehend that this tall, powerfully built man before her was the man she had married that afternoon.

Harshly Brice caught hold of her again. Noting her apprehension, he obviously believed she was putting on an act. 'Don't tell me you've never seen a naked man before.'

Not the way he implied. Without thinking, she whispered, 'No,' but he didn't appear to be listening. With a soothing hand he brushed back her tumbled hair. 'You don't have to be frightened. I'm not a brute,' he said.

As she stirred uneasily, his arms tightened and he

brought her closer to the abrasive roughness of his chest. Bending his head, while her breath caught, he trailed warm lips from her cheek to her ear and down her neck. Macy felt the room begin to whirl and her trembling increased as her breathing became slow and laboured.

Unable to protest against the dictates of her clamorous senses, her own arms slid feverishly around his broad shoulders, her nails digging in his flesh as sensation rioted through her. His mouth continued to explore her body, sending thrills of sensuous pleasure to every part of her. In a moment of sanity she knew a brief twinge of shame that she was responding so avidly when he didn't love her but her remorse didn't last as her passion mounted eagerly to meet his.

'You're beautiful!' he muttered, gathering her up and settling with her on the wide bed. 'You're so slim and pliant even to look at you threatens to drive me insane.'

Macy merely moaned as his lips moved against her mouth. She no longer wanted to cringe from him. Her only fear now was that he might leave her. That this might be just another step in his determination to punish her. He might go so far and stop. Then, catching a glimpse of his burning eyes, she realised that, for this one night at any rate, this was far from his intention.

'The first time I saw you I wanted you,' he said thickly.

Want? Macy rejected the word sharply then paused. Wasn't she as guilty as he? Hadn't she felt the same electric current between them immediately—if she hadn't understood it as clearly as Brice? She quivered, feeling it piercing her again as he levered himself on an elbow to stare down on her. She had to have him. Nothing else mattered, so how could she criticise his needs when they were so identical to her own?

As if her shudder was a sign he had been waiting for, Brice slid his fingers to the fastening of her bra and swiftly took it off, his movements not nearly as patient as they had been. With quick expertise he removed her panties while his lips plundered her full throbbing breasts. She moaned deep in her throat, her mind clouding with devastation when his hand again slid to the base of her spine, drawing her slender body ruthlessly up to him so she could feel the hardness of his very bones. Then, as he lifted his head from her breasts, her arms went convulsively round his neck and her parted lips met his halfway.

The shock of his mouth, this time, sent her over the bounds of reason. She felt the tremor running through him as every beat in her body stampeded apace and her blood leapt to vibrant life. Emotion choked her as their lips clung, becoming a single entity, a vortex of burning hunger. There was a relentless fever running in her blood which evoked a response to Brice's caresses that bordered on wildness.

'I have to have every bit of you,' he said savagely, but she no longer tried to deny him. How could she when every bit of her was crying out for him? His lips were warm and moist and she whimpered with pleasure and pressed herself unashamedly against him. Ever since she had known him she had wanted to be with him like this but she had never dared admit it, not even to herself. But before it had been almost wholly curiosity. She would never have believed that being so close to a man could bring her to such a pitch of ecstasy. Brice wasn't any man, of course, he was her husband. But she knew she could have married a hundred other men and never felt like this. She was consumed by such a volume of desire that it scarcely seemed to matter that he didn't care for her any more.

Gathering her softness ever closer, his voice became thick and inarticulate, the things he muttered against her heated skin, barely decipherable. Macy's slender body began writhing under his as he explored her mouth deeply, letting their body temperatures rise simultaneously until eventually there was no control. Macy was only vaguely aware of her pleading strangled cry in a voice she barely recognised as her own.

Initially Brice was gentle, pausing abruptly at her surprised whimper of pain, waiting until it passed. Then, as though some kind of uncontrollable urgency shook him, with hot kisses and impatient hands he possessed her completely. As she absorbed him into her, their bodies welded and the feeling within them rose to a wild crescendo. They had shared turmoil, now they shared total intimacy. Macy felt something powerful inside her burning her up as Brice held her tightly to him as she was exposed to the increasing strength of his unleashed emotions.

As waves of passion coursed through Macy, her movements became more and more uninhibited. Responding to his demands with feverish abandonment she was like a flame in his arms. Then, when she thought she had touched the very pinnacle of desire, like an unpremeditated explosion of the elements, a shower of white hot ecstasy spread through her entirely, just as Brice shuddered violently against her.

When he spoke to her soon afterwards, she was still drifting beyond the realms of reality but with a satisfied warmth in her body instead of the hunger that he had so wonderfully appeased.

'Are you all right?' he asked.

Why was his voice unsteady, she wondered, nodding dreamily.

'Hi!' His knuckles nuzzled her cooling cheek. 'You aren't going to sleep on me, are you?'

Drowsily she blinked. 'I do feel sleepy.'

Incredibly he suggested, 'A shower will wake you up.'

'Why?' Her eyes opened wide.

'You'll see,' he smiled.

While her pulse began racing again, he picked her up, carrying her through to the bathroom with no noticeable strain to his strong, lithe body. Macy steadied herself as he tucked her long hair under a plastic cap and turned on the water. Drawing her into the shower beside him, he stood with his arms around her under the powerful jet until they were both soaked. Macy had to keep her eyes closed under the force of the water but she was achingly conscious of Brice's bare wet skin against her own. Each time he moved against her she experienced desires which she had thought fully satisfied, at least for the time being.

Eventually he guided her out, and when she groped blindly for a towel, rather than look at the naked magnificence of his body, he took one from a rail and wrapped it round her.

'I only half-believed you were a virgin,' he said, as he began drying her. He did it very slowly and caressingly and soon she was longing for him to dispense with the towel and to stroke her bare flesh.

'I've never slept with a man before,' she murmured, her cheeks hot. 'Does it matter?'

'I like to know you're all mine.' His eyes went over her, disturbingly hard and possessive as he suddenly flung the towel away and carried her back to bed.

Soon he was driving her mindless again and she clung to him, responding to him passionately as he left her in no doubt as to how much she aroused him. But this time his hands were gentler as they moved tenderly over her swelling breasts. When she began involuntarily to caress him, he told her how to please him and if she was slow to begin with, he didn't seem displeased with her lack of practice. But he didn't give her much time to learn as his own reciprocal movements filled her with exquisite delight, and when he took her again there was no way she could hide the completeness of her surrender.

It seemed a long time before he let her rest. Macy was sure dawn was approaching when he turned her comfortably in his arms and she drifted off to sleep. Her last recollection was of his kiss on her shoulder, his hands on her breasts. Next morning, when she stirred, she expected to find him beside her and stretched out her hand with her first drowsy thoughts to touch him, but he wasn't there. She encountered only empty space. With a start of dismay, her eyes flew open but her panic subsided as she saw him standing by the window.

He was formally dressed, an obvious indication that he was going to the factory. Macy sighed. She had been hoping he might, for once, relax his busy schedule and spend one day with her. As he had obviously no intention of staying at home, she tried not to be disappointed. He had a job to do and she didn't doubt he was conscientious. Come to that, hadn't she a job to do herself? Shouldn't she be up getting his breakfast?

'Brice?' she murmured with a tender smile.

He turned quickly, meeting her tenderness with a cold frown. 'I thought you'd sleep all morning.'

'You should have woken me up,' she began to get out of bed until she suddenly realised she had nothing on and pulled the sheet over her again.

Expecting a teasing remark about it being rather late for modesty, she was startled that he appeared to appreciate her nakedness no more than she did. With a savage twist of his sensuous mouth, he lifted his robe from the back of a nearby chair and tossed it to her.

'Wear that,' he snapped.

Macy stared at him as she automatically grabbed hold of it. 'Is something wrong?' she asked nervously.

'Nothing more than usual.'

As she wriggled from under the sheet into the robe, she considered his odd remark. What did he mean? 'Trouble at the works?'

'No business is ever without it.'

Biting her lip, Macy suddenly sensed he was shutting her out, yet after the night they had just spent, she couldn't believe it. Go carefully, a voice warned faintly but she took notice.

Instead of asking him bluntly if she had annoyed him

in some way, she smiled cheerfully and said, 'I'll get your breakfast.'

'I've had it.'

Her heart sank. 'You're sure?'

He looked impatient at her persistence. 'It's not something I'd lie about.'

'I'm sorry.' She glanced at his dark face uncertainly, 'I promise I won't sleep in tomorrow. What time will you be home?'

'I can't say.'

Were all men who went to business so short in the mornings? Her father had worked at home so she didn't know. Tying the robe which almost swamped her, so tightly round her waist that it threatened her breathing, she stepped nearer her husband. If she wasn't to see him all day she had to be close to him for even a few seconds. He couldn't be in all that much of a hurry?

Stopping within inches of him, she tossed back her long hair smiled at him lovingly but he only regarded her stonily and stepped aside. Macy felt too stunned to move for a moment. Brice's eyes were glacial and he was pale. It seemed clear that he wanted nothing more to do with her.

'What is it?' she choked, turning to him desperately, 'Didn't I p-please you, last night?'

He reached for his jacket with no pity for her hot cheeks. 'If you imagine that last night has changed my opinion of you, Macy, you're mistaken. What happened then makes no difference to the situation at all and the sooner you realise this, my sweet, the easier you'll find it to reconcile yourself to the inevitable.'

Macy stared at him, the colour draining from her face. As he spoke, disbelief exploded through her head and, stunned by shock, she swayed. Lifting his hands, as if to help her, he let them fall again, watching dispassionately, though a nerve jumped in the tightness of his jaw, as she regained her balance without his help.

'You have your aunt to visit,' he reminded her coldly

while she was still trying to find her voice. 'You have your car?'

Macy nodded. He hadn't forgotten Kate, which was kind of him. And maybe he didn't really mean all the cruel things he said? Deliberately thrusting all thoughts of his harshness from her, she whispered gratefully, 'She'll be looking forward to seeing me.'

His face hardened further, as though he was steeling himself against the appeal in her eyes. 'Don't stay too long, will you? Not until you're sure of your way home.'

Gazing after him, as he abruptly left the room, some of Macy's hard won composure slipped as she wondered if he would ever forgive her? She wouldn't want to face the future without him now, but how could she ever hope to survive if he didn't?

With a weary shrug she decided to get dressed and look over the house to see if there was anything to do before she left to visit Kate. She didn't know how domesticated Brice was. There might be breakfast dishes to wash and the fridge would be to check to see if there was anything for dinner? He could have overlooked such things as provisions. He hadn't mentioned what time he would be back, that evening, but she was sure he would ring and tell her, once he knew what he was doing?

Suddenly, as she glanced around the bedroom, she realised it had been freshly decorated. Brice must have had the painters in when they had finished the outside. If it wasn't exactly what she might have chosen herself, the lightly patterned wallpaper blended well with the satin-finished furniture, which also looked new. He had obviously thrown all the old stuff out and she wished she had noticed last night. But then, last night, he hadn't given her a chance to notice anything but himself.

Trying not to remember the blissful hours she had spent in his arms, she made the bed and dressed quickly in a sweater and jeans. Tying back her thick hair, still damp from her hurried shower, she was surprised to see she looked exactly the same as she'd looked yesterday. This morning there was a beautiful bloom to her cheeks but her eyes were still faintly shadowed. She must stop being so anxious, she told herself firmly. Brice would be home again soon and by then he might feel differently about everything. It didn't seem possible that he would never learn to trust her again.

CHAPTER SEVEN

RUNNING downstairs, Macy was determined to ignore her aching doubts and to lose herself completely in the day ahead. She had lost count of the times she had told herself that Brice must care a little yet she repeated it again and again. If she was patient there was everything to be gained.

At the foot of the stairs she was startled to the point of being almost frightened, on hearing what sounded like someone moving around in the kitchen. Thinking it could only be Brice come back for something, she was on her way to investigate when the phone rang. Not knowing which to see to first, she grabbed the phone as it was nearest.

'Mrs Sinclair.' The number of the house went clean out of her head so she had to give her name.

'Helping to spread the news already, are you?' a deep voice mocked.

No one had a voice like him. It went right down to her toes, curling them convulsively. 'Brice!' she gasped 'Where are you?'

'In my office at the moment,' he replied, 'with an impatient secretary waiting to get on with the mail. I forgot to mention earlier that you'll find a Mrs Bland in the kitchen. I thought I'd better give you a ring.'

Oh! Relief flooded Macy but anger as well. 'I wish you hadn't forgotten to tell me, Brice. I've just come down and got such a fright when I heard someone moving around ...'

He made no apology. 'I'm a busy man, Macy. If some domestic detail escapes me, don't make a fuss.'

A fuss? He had a nerve! Anybody could have been in the kitchen! 'Who is Mrs Bland, anyway?' she asked sarcastically.

'She used to be Alec's housekeeper. I merely said she could carry on.'

'But we don't need her.'

'Yes we do,' he retorted curtly. 'I married you, Macy, for the sake of the firm, but I don't intend that such a sacrifice should go wholly unrewarded. Mrs Bland will do the cooking and housekeeping. Your job is to keep me happy—and I don't want a wife who is too tired of an evening to do that.'

The dropping of his receiver was quiet but sounded very final. Despair hit Macy afresh and very hard. A cleaning firm—now a housekeeper. Next, she shouldn't wonder, there'd be a gardener! She had come to see her new home as a kind of substitute for the career she'd been forced to give up. Now, she saw such dreams fast disappearing. Brice didn't want an adoring young wife. He wanted one with no claim on his emotions and his life arranged so that if ever he tired of her, he would scarcely notice her going!

Dully, Macy made her way to the kitchen. This day, which she had hoped might turn out to be wonderful, wasn't even having a good beginning.

The woman by the sink turned as Macy pushed open the kitchen door. She was in late middle-age and looked at Macy with eyes which never revealed her feelings. 'Mrs Sinclair?'

'Yes, Mrs Bland.' Macy smiled, determined to be friendly.

Mrs Bland didn't smile back but she didn't frown either. She had the look of a woman who knew her place and wouldn't dream of leaving it. 'You'll be wanting breakfast, Madam, I expect?'

Macy grimaced inwardly. She had never been called Madam in her life. 'Just coffee, Mrs Bland, thank you. And the name's Macy.'

Mrs Bland shook her head disapprovingly. 'I'm sorry, ma'am, I never get that familiar with my employers.'

Macy tried again. 'My husband just rang. He'd forgotten to mention you were here. He said you worked for Mr Pearson?'

'Fifteen years,' the woman sighed. 'He was very easy to do with. He even slept on the ground floor so as to save me the stairs.'

'We've a cleaning firm coming in,' Macy hastened to inform her. 'They'll do upstairs so you still won't need to bother.' She didn't add that she intended looking after the master-bedroom herself.

Mrs Bland nodded but didn't seem that impressed. 'Some of these firms are more bother than they're worth,' she grumbled.

Macy quickly drank the coffee Mrs Bland poured and said she would be out for the rest of the day. 'I'm not sure what time my husband will be home,' she remembered to mention before she left. 'He might ring and tell you?'

'Six o'clock. That's what he said anyway,' Mrs Bland muttered, turning back to her sink so that she didn't notice Macy's hurt expression.

Kate was pleased to see her. She had been happy, with the quiet contentment of those who have had their last wishes granted, ever since Macy had told her she was marrying Brice. If for no other reason, her marriage had been worth it for what it had done for Kate, Macy decided, kissing her aunt's cheek.

'Your wedding was wonderful,' Kate sighed. 'I only wish you could have gone away for a few days.'

Macy pinned a rueful smile on her lips. 'Brice can't spare time from the mill.' Kate always called the factory the mill. 'He works hard.'

'You can tell,' Kate smiled. 'He has the look of a man who always has, but you should try and see that he learns to relax.'

Macy picked up one of her aunt's favourite books. T.V. tired her now but she loved having Macy read aloud to her. 'We'll have a honeymoon as soon as he gets things sorted out,' she promised, sitting down in the chair by Kate's bed and opening the book.

During the next few weeks, Macy visited Kate daily, apart from weekends, but she stopped using her car. Brice wasn't aware of this and it was fairly easy to deceive him, if only by saying nothing. They both went to see Kate on Sundays and he always took her in his car.

Macy's small run-about was parked in the smaller of the two garages that adjoined the house. This was why Brice hadn't noticed she wasn't taking it out. About a week after they were married, she realised she hadn't enough money to spare for petrol. Worse than this, there wasn't enough left to pay Miss Kirby. Not being able to pay Miss Kirby had proved a terrible blow. It had been days before she'd managed to pluck up sufficient courage to tell Brice, and though he had undertaken to remunerate Miss Kirby for her services, in addition to the night nurse, it had not been before he'd received a detailed statement of the money she had spent.

Macy, painfully aware of his anger, had been determined not to add to it, or invite further humiliation by asking for anything for herself. When she thought of all he was doing for Kate—he had even asked her to live with them, though she had refused— she couldn't find it in her heart to condemn him in any way.

But the fact remained that she could no longer afford to run her car, so Macy used the bus. Nor did she consider herself ill-treated in any way. Brice could have had her arrested, or at least dismissed from the factory with her reputation in shreds. Instead he had given her his name and kept her in comfort and looked after her family as well. It made such a small thing as no pocket money seem nothing by comparison.

They had been married for over five weeks before Brice found out about the car. One late afternoon she was caught in a downpour, both before and after catching the bus, and arrived home wet through. The bus had been late, too, which hadn't helped matters. It made her late and she was soaking in a hot bath when Brice came home.

He must be early! Macy frowned as she glanced at the time. It was after six but he wasn't usually home until nearer seven. She had hoped to be out before he returned. She didn't mind him seeing her in the bath, it was a huge tub and he sometimes joined her, but she had been so wet and cold that she had left her clothes on the floor and didn't want him to see them.

'Macy?' he strode into the bathroom for she hadn't locked the door, then he stopped short, as his glance fell on her wet things. For a moment he paused as though shocked, then, stopping, he picked up her dripping jumper. 'Is this yours?'

'Yes.' She forced a light laugh. 'I got wet.'

'Obviously.' His grey eyes iced. 'What I want to know is how and where?'

She ought to be getting used to how he could rap out questions. 'Coming home.'

Sceptically his mouth twisted. 'Did the roof blow off your car?'

Still trying to avoid the issue, she retorted. 'It's been raining. You didn't think I'd been rolling in wet grass?'

'How would I know?' In disgust he flung the wet jumper back on the tiles and positioned himself on the edge of the bath.

'Why don't you join me?' she asked, the softness of her voice concealing her real purpose to stop him asking questions. This was the first time she had deliberately tried to take advantage of the sexual magnetism between them. In the weeks of their marriage, Brice's contempt for her hadn't changed but in bed their relationship was entirely satisfactory. Often, she sensed, it made him angry that her body had such a hold over him, for all he tried to fight it. And fight it, she was sure he did. Frequently, during the night, she would wake to find him reaching for her and then turning abruptly away. Then, following a few minutes' silent struggle, he would turn again to take her in his arms with a groan of surrender she wasn't supposed to hear. Sometimes his frustration would be reflected in the near violence of his lovemaking, but whether he was rough or gentle the outcome was the same. He always wanted more. Instead of decreasing, his passion for her—though this was maybe all it was—grew more demanding each day.

Sitting up straighter in the bath, ignoring the twinges of self-consciousness which still occasionally plagued her, Macy let the bath foam that covered her slowly disperse to reveal the rosy tips of her breasts. Beneath her lowered lids, she saw both his jaw and hands clench as he stared at her, absorbing her against his will.

'You'd better get out of there, Macy,' he said tersely, 'I want an explanation for all this.' His toe touched her wet clothes. 'And I've news for you about this evening.'

'I can tell you and you can tell me,' she teased, her blue eyes playful, 'just as easily in here.'

'No!' he exploded, bending to lift her ruthlessly out himself, careless of the impeccable suit he was wearing. Reaching for a towel he threw it around her steaming, provocative body, his breathing slightly rougher and dull coins of red on his cheeks.

As Macy gasped at the suddenness of her transition she noticed a muscle jerk at the side of his mouth and wondered why he tried so hard to keep her at a distance.

'Get dressed,' he commanded shortly, avoiding her wistful glance. 'I'll be back in a minute.'

Macy dried herself slowly, her movements lethargic. After she finished, she wandered into the bedroom. Suddenly she felt tired and wondered if Brice would mind if she lay down for a while. No, that wouldn't be a good idea. If he thought it was an invitation, she mightn't get any rest. And once in his arms, she was as eager to make love as he was.

Brice returned, scattering her sensuous thoughts with a face like thunder. 'Why haven't you been using your car?' he demanded. 'I've just been to the garage and found it covered with cobwebs. There's dust an inch thick, too. Is there something wrong with it?'

'I hadn't any petrol,' she confessed, dismayed by what he had discovered but knowing better than to continue withholding the truth. 'It doesn't matter,' she hastened. 'The bus is quite convenient.'

His eyes sparked dangerously. 'What the hell are you talking about, Macy? Why didn't you get some petrol?'

Drawing the sash of her robe tighter, Macy cautiously licked dry lips. 'I've been getting short of money...'

He laughed sarcastically. 'You can certainly get through it.'

Stung, she retorted, 'Since you won't let me earn any and it doesn't grow on trees...'

He looked as if he could have hit her. 'Now you can't sell your work to unscrupulous buyers, you expect me...'

'No, I don't!' she interrupted, soft mouth taut. 'If you hadn't brought this up, I'd never have mentioned it. You provide me with board and lodgings and pay people to look after Kate. I feel I'm getting more than enough.'

'So do I,' he said grimly.

Out of the corner of her eye, as she sat down at the dressing-table, Macy watched him pacing the room. He was super-charged with restless energy. She wondered where he got it from. His vitality was amazing. He could work an eighteen-hour day and still come home and wake her up.

'What did you wish to speak to me about?' she asked with a sigh.

He seemed to hesitate over changing the subject then

resignedly shrugged his shoulders. 'Some American friends of mine are here and anxious to meet you.'

'Do you want them to meet me?'

Her emphasis that it was his opinion that interested her, hardened his eyes. 'I wouldn't have mentioned it otherwise. They want us to have dinner with them.'

'What shall I wear?' She was learning that it didn't hurt so much if she didn't probe too hard into the reasons behind his actions. 'I haven't anything new.'

'We can't do anything about that now,' he retorted. 'Fortunately you happen to be very lovely. Whatever you wear doesn't seem to make any difference.'

Macy glanced at him with a radiant smile then paused. She must stop drinking in every kind word he said to her as if she was dying of thirst. Her smile fading, she got to her feet to search for her red dress in the wardrobe. He watched silently as she sorted through her clothes then turned to get ready himself.

As they drove to the hotel where his friends were staying, she asked, 'Wouldn't you like to invite them to Northholt?'

'They're not here for long,' Brice explained. 'But we can see what they're doing tomorrow. It might be a good idea, if you think Mrs Bland is up to it.'

'I can help as well,' she reminded him dryly. Mrs Bland, she was sure, could cope with anything. During the weeks she had been with them, Macy was no nearer getting to know her but she never doubted her competence. Macy couldn't fault her over the least little thing. She was always polite and obliging but it was like living with a machine—and she was just about as much company!

Brice's friends consisted of two couples perhaps a few years older than himself. Macy learned that they also shared business interests and were curious to know what was keeping Brice in England. They made no secret that they had been surprised to hear of his sudden marriage but neither did they try and hide that they were charmed by his beautiful bride.

The obvious sincerity of the compliments she was paid helped Macy's bruised confidence a lot. It came to her that Brice wouldn't have invited her to meet his friends if he hadn't, in some way, been proud of her. He gave no hint that their marriage wasn't a normal one. In fact he did everything he could to give the impression it was an extremely happy one. For a few hours Macy basked in his warm smiles and thrilled as his hand continually sought hers or found its way round her waist. He was putting on an act, of course, but she wouldn't have been human if she hadn't responded and wanted to make the most of it. Frequently she found herself thinking how wonderful it would have been if the love he pretended to have for her had been real.

After dining, they went on to a nightclub and danced. Macy enjoyed this part of the evening very much, especially when she danced with Brice. Her body was full of rhythm, she moved with a natural grace and abandon which betrayed her passionate nature and had his eyes smouldering as they circled the floor together. The clean scent of Brice's skin and the power of his muscles against her, stirred Macy unbearably. Soon she became curiously light-headed and though he teased in her ear that she'd had too much champagne, evidence that he wasn't wholly undisturbed himself soon became increasingly apparent.

Just after twelve they left, after inviting the Americans to dinner at Northholt the following evening, an invitation which was promptly accepted.

'We didn't have to hurry away,' Macy assured Brice as he got in the car beside her. 'I was quite willing to stay longer.'

'I wasn't,' he growled, before starting the car, catching her closely against his chest, his mouth covering hers in a kiss of sheer hunger. 'I didn't know how much longer I could hold out. I'm still not sure, come to that.'

Later, in the more comfortable privacy of their

bedroom, he undressed her swiftly. Usually he liked to take his time over this, teasing and tantalising her until she was weak and dizzy with desire, but tonight he was oddly impatient. His own clothes were removed just as swiftly.

'You're trembling,' he said thickly.

It wouldn't be the first time! 'I'm cold,' she excused, wrapping her arms around his neck.

He laughed softly and once more his lips closed over hers as he carried her to the bed. There he moulded her pliant curves to the hardness of his big body, exploring every inch of her, only breaking off to cover her face and throat with soft, burning kisses. Macy shuddered against him as his hands possessively caressed her pink-tipped breasts before sliding demandingly over her flat stomach to her thighs.

'I want you,' he muttered. 'All of you.'

She swallowed hard, her heart beating wildly. 'You usually take what you want.'

'You can be sure,' he said hoarsely.

Their first dinner party was a success, as Macy had known it would be. Mrs Bland didn't turn a hair at being asked to provide a meal for four extra guests at such short notice. She informed Macy that Mr Pearson had occasionally brought guests home for dinner with no notice at all, and when Macy suggested a menu, she said they had all the ingredients in the house. She allowed Macy to assist with very little; she even brought a friend in to help serve the meal.

The drawing room looked very nice. Macy ran an appraising eye over it. She had made new covers for the chairs and sofa which was a definite improvement on the old brown velvet. The dining room looked nice too. She had insisted on setting the table herself and considered she had made a good job of it. Brice had commissioned the painters and decorators to continue the work he had started on their bedroom and it was finished as far as he declared it was sensible to go until he decided whether or not he would return to the States. A gardening contractor had also been engaged and while Macy had to admit he had worked wonders in an incredibly short time, she still wished she had been able to do it herself.

Life, after the dinner party, went on much the same as usual, apart from one thing. Macy became frequently aware of a vague feeling of malaise. Her aunt's health was worsening rapidly now and Macy blamed the extra worry as the reason for not feeling so good. The tedious journey to see Kate she found increasingly tiring, and if she could have borne to sacrifice the only real closeness she had with Brice, which was in bed, she might have tried to persuade him to allow her to stay at her aunt's some nights.

Brice didn't mention her car again, nor did he offer her any alternative form of transport. Believing it was yet another way he was using to punish her, Macy accepted her struggles to catch and connect buses on three different routes without complaint. The problem of having no money to spend on personal things bothered her but didn't really hurt until she found she could no longer afford to buy a small present for Kate. Not even a bunch of flowers. The garden at Northholt wasn't blooming yet, neither did any of their neighbours appear to be. Most of the residents in the street were elderly and too concerned over making ends meet on dwindling incomes to bother very much with their gardens.

It was Miss Kirby who indirectly solved her problems when she mentioned how her niece, who ran a florists, was having trouble finding someone reliable to deliver her flowers. When she went on to say it was only for a couple of hours each morning, Macy impulsively asked if she thought her niece would consider taking her on? She managed to smooth the doubt from Miss Kirby's face by hastily improvising that Brice was having some difficulty taking over Mr Pearson's firm and earning even a little money of her own would help.

'I'm sure Wendy would welcome you with open arms,' Miss Kirby smiled, Macy's explanation sounding perfectly feasible. 'I'll see her this evening.'

Thus, Macy found herself employed for approximately two hours a day. The hours suited her as she could go straight from the flower shop to see Kate before going home again. She had been forced to ask Miss Kirby not to say anything about her job to Kate for fear she mentioned it to Brice. She pretended she didn't want him to know in case he disapproved of her working.

Everything went well until the day the van she drove got a flat tyre. This, in itself, wasn't such a terrible thing, but because she couldn't change the wheel herself, she had to wait for a garage to come and do it for her. Which made her over an hour late. It was nearly one when she made her last delivery of a dozen red roses to a hotel near the city centre. She was standing outside it, checking she had the right address, when to her surprise, Tim Matthews, one of the young executives from Pearsons, bumped into her, nearly knocking her down.

'Good Lord!' he cried, halting in the middle of an involuntary apology as his hands flew out to catch her. 'Macy, it's you!'

'Hello, Tim.' She couldn't help smiling at his sheer astonishment. 'I'm not a ghost.'

'I don't think a ghost would have given me such a fright,' he laughed. 'You're the last person I expected to see. The news of your wedding is all over the factory but you seemed to have disappeared. I don't suppose your old friends are good enough for you now,' he teased. 'Now that you're married to the boss!'

He still held her clasped lightly to him and she glanced at him uncertainly. Tim had taken her out several times before Kate had become ill, but when he had fallen in love with her she had let their friendship cool after she realised she couldn't return his feelings. He was nice though. Too nice to snub by just walking away and ignoring him.

'Brice sort of rushed me off my feet,' she murmured, awkwardly. 'And with my aunt being so ill, he thought it would be better if we were married quietly. He didn't want me to go on working.'

'If you'd been my wife I wouldn't have wanted you to go on working either,' Tim sighed. 'However, no matter how green I am with envy, my love, I'm still going to wish you the best of everything.' Then, before Macy had time to move, he pulled her closer and kissed her.

Because Tim was intent on what he was doing and got somewhat carried away, and Macy was trying tactfully to stop him, neither of them noticed the taxi drawing up beside them and Brice and two men getting out. Macy didn't see her husband glance idly in her direction then pause abruptly to request his two guests to go on ahead. The first indication she had of his presence was when his icy voice tore Tim and her apart.

'Just what's going on?' he exclaimed.

Tim, usually garrulous, for the second time in minutes, seemed completely at a loss for words, while Macy, wondering hollowly where on earth Brice had sprung from, stood staring at him, her cheeks as red as the roses she was clutching.

'Don't try and find excuses,' Brice snapped at her, his eyes cold with anger. 'You look as guilty as hell.' With a quick movement of his hand, before she had a chance to guess his intentions, he whipped the roses from her arms and flung them into a nearby bin. Macy watched, horrified, as two young boys snatched them out again and ran off with them, whooping with glee.

'Oh, Brice, you don't know what you've done!' she gasped.

'Let that be a warning to the next fool who buys you flowers,' he retorted, turning furiously to a still speechless Tim. 'As for you, Matthews, if you value your very good job you'd better stay away from my wife.'

Tim went as white as the best brand of paint. 'I'm sorry, old man . . .' he began.

'Don't "old man" me!' Brice rapped, his glare clearly indicating that though he was a few years older, if they'd been in a less public place he'd have taken the greatest pleasure in knocking the other man down.

Macy tried to intervene but was told curtly by Brice to shut up. Icily he continued talking to Tim. 'John Noble and David Lewin from General Textiles are waiting for me inside the hotel. I was taking them for lunch. As you won't have anything better to do now, you can go and entertain them while I go home with my wife.'

He took her all the way by taxi, insisting on accompanying her though she protested she could manage herself.

His eyes were hard as he refused to listen to her attempts to reason with him. 'Do you think I'm going to give you a chance to double back and join your lover? You must take me for a fool.'

'Tim isn't my lover,' she retorted, when she could trust herself to speak.

'Not your lover?' he jeered grimly. 'If he isn't, then what were you doing in his arms, in the middle of a city street? You'll be trying to tell me next that you don't know him!'

'No.'

'You used to go out with him?'

There seemed no sense in denying it. 'Yes,' she replied despondently. 'Two years ago.'

'And you think you can take up where you left off?'

Brice was being totally impossible. Macy glanced at him despairingly, blinking back tears. She wanted to save her job but she realised it might be her job or Tim's. 'Tim isn't involved with me,' she said flatly. 'We just bumped into each other, this morning, accidentally. He kissed me but it was just his way of wishing me all the best as he hasn't seen me since I was married.'

'And the flowers?' Brice taunted mockingly, 'How do you propose explaining them?'

She had hoped he had forgotten about the ill-fated roses and flushed guiltily. 'They had nothing to do with Tim.'

His mouth tightened. 'Where did they come from, then, if it wasn't from him?'

Macy sighed futilely, controlling a quiver of apprehension. With Brice it never paid to try and evade the truth. Bitterly she muttered, 'I told you, I can explain.'

'Later,' he said curtly, as the taxi drew up outside Northholt and he became aware of the curious driver. Cynically he lowered his voice as he ordered her not to leave the house. 'I'll be back as soon as I can,' he snapped.

'I have to go to Kate's,' Macy paused in dismay as she got out, wondering how she could have forgotten. 'I should go now,' she pleaded anxiously as Brice shook his head. 'She'll be expecting me and I promise I won't see Tim.'

'You won't get the chance,' Brice's voice had icicles dripping off it. 'I'll be keeping him right under my eye during lunch and I'm coming straight home afterwards. As for Kate, I'll take you to visit her this evening, if I haven't murdered you first.'

Macy didn't feel like lunch. As she trailed into the house, she hoped sullenly that Brice's lunch choked him! She could imagine poor Tim, sitting shivering while Brice glared at him, being punished for crimes he had never committed. She would only concede that Brice might have had some excuse for jumping to the wrong conclusions.

There was no one in the kitchen. Mrs Bland was usually in her own quarters at this time of day. Listlessly

Macy made herself a cup of tea, drinking it by the telephone as she checked that Kate was all right and assured Miss Kirby she would be there later. Then she rang Miss Kirby's niece at the flower shop. When she got through she still had no clear idea what she was going to say.

Having already been in touch with Wendy about the flat tyre, she offered some jumbled excuse about not feeling well and having to come home. She told her where the van was parked and Wendy said she wasn't to worry, she would send someone round to pick it up. She sounded so sympathetic that Macy was sorely tempted to confess what had really happened, but she still hoped that Brice might be persuaded to allow her to keep her job and Wendy might be none the wiser.

It was after four when Brice returned, still in a bad mood. Macy tried not to imagine what conclusions his guests had come to.

She was in their bedroom when he arrived, but not by intent, as he appeared to think. She had come up to rinse her face and hands having spent the afternoon in the lounge, trying to think of some way by which she could keep her job without continuing to deceive him.

'I thought I would find you here,' he sneered, 'but you needn't think you can use your sexy body this time to get round me. I've been watching you for further signs of cheating and you'll have to be very good indeed to talk your way out of this one!'

His mood wasn't bad—it was filthy! 'What do you mean—cheating?' she gasped.

'You aren't that dumb!' he countered furiously. 'If Matthews isn't your lover, he could only have been paying you for something. For his sake, I hope not!'

'That's ridiculous!' she burst out.

'Is it?' he retorted, eyes burning into her. 'Does he know anything about those designs you sold?'

Macy stared at him in dismay, blinking back tears. There was no other way, she would have to tell him, but what hurt was this proof of his ever-festering mistrust.

'Tim Matthews knows nothing of my ill-gotten gains,' she replied bitterly, 'and I wasn't selling him anything. And, as I said before, he isn't my lover.'

'Isn't,' Brice snapped, 'but he could have been?'

'You must know that couldn't be true,' she retorted angrily. 'Nor was that kind of relationship between us ever suggested, when I went out with him.'

'I saw how he looked at you,' Brice said sharply. 'Don't tell me he wasn't keen. Why did you break up?'

What had this to do with what happened this afternoon? Macy wanted to refuse to explain but she dared not, not with Brice looking at her with such enmity.

'He was getting too fond of me,' she confessed reluctantly. 'I didn't think it right to encourage him.'

'Wasn't he wealthy enough?'

Because of the roundabout hint this contained, she went pale and didn't answer.

'So . . .' he taunted, eyes like gimlets, 'before you lose your tongue completely, how about the roses? How do you intend explaining them away?'

'There's a quite simple explanation,' she mumbled, wishing desperately that he had never seen her with them. But, after all, he couldn't stop her working—or could he? When her tortured mind refused to answer optimistically, she gulped and continued, 'I'm working, part time, for a florist. I deliver flowers.'

'You—what!'

'It's not a crime!' she defended bravely, trying not to shrink from his furious hostility. 'I work hard and get paid the going rate. My employer is very good to me.'

'I can imagine!' Brice snarled, his voice hard with rage. He had been keeping his distance. Now he was so close she could see the leaping sparks in his eyes. 'I just can't take this in,' he grated, savagely grabbing her shoulders, 'It doesn't seem possible, that you deliberately sought employment when I forbade you . . .'

'You forbade me to design!'

He was incensed that she dared try and defend herself. 'Anything that puts you in contact with a susceptible public.'

She blanched. 'You can't mean that!'

'I do!'

She almost gave up. She was obviously wasting time yet she was driven to appeal, 'I only wanted to earn a little money, Brice. Pocket money, if you like...'

He mightn't have heard her. Though he was clearly making an effort to calm himself, his breath still rasped. 'My wife delivering flowers!' He was taking it like a personal affront. 'You don't care how much you humiliate me, do you? I suppose this is your way of seeking revenge because I made you marry me?'

'I wasn't seeking revenge,' she denied quickly. 'And I don't see how you could be humiliated, Brice. Plenty of married women work...'

'I won't have you working,' he said coldly. 'I might have felt differently if I'd been married to someone else but I'd never know what you were up to. How did you deliver your flowers, by the way? Did you walk?'

'No, I had a van,' she replied bitterly, as all the old hurt returned.

'I didn't see any van,' he frowned.

'You wouldn't. It was parked in a side-street.'

Brice's face grew even grimmer. 'And what did your boss say when you told him what had happened?'

'When I told her what had happened, you mean.'

'Come again?'

Macy explained wearily. 'My boss is—was, a woman.'

She felt the hands on her shoulders relax slightly but his eyes were no kinder as he snapped. 'I damn well hope she had the sense to dismiss you instantly.'

CHAPTER EIGHT

MACY retorted mutinously. 'Well she didn't! When I explained, she was very nice.'

Brice's dark brows rose. 'Even when she learned you'd abandoned the van?'

'She's sending someone to pick it up.'

'And the roses? She can't have been so pleased over what happened to them?'

Blue eyes darkening helplessly, Macy confessed tautly. 'I didn't tell her. I'm a coward! I kept trying to think of something and in the end, when I couldn't, instead of telling the truth I let her think I'd delivered them.'

'For once your inventive little mind let you down?'

Macy's face flushed with distress. 'I'll have to tell her, of course.'

Letting go of her abruptly, Brice reached in his pocket for his cheque book. 'The name of your boss?' he demanded curtly, and when Macy told him, he wrote out a cheque and handed it to her. 'Send that—along with your resignation,' he snapped. 'Address it now, before you forget, and we'll post it on our way to your aunt's. She'll receive it in the morning.'

'But I can't let Wendy down like this!' Macy protested. 'She's expecting me in the morning. She won't be able to find anyone else at such short notice.'

'When she sees what I've sent,' Brice drawled suavely, 'I'm sure she will forgive you.'

Glancing abstractedly at the slip of paper he had thrust in her hand, Macy gasped. It was more than she would have earned in a month!

'I added a little extra in lieu of notice, to cover any inconvenience,' he smiled as she stared at him.

131

Suddenly incensed by his taunting smile, Macy wildly clasped his arm. 'Don't you see?' she cried. 'I need this job! If I can't do what I'm trained for, I have to do something—and it's not easy to get anything!'

'Indeed!' his eyes suddenly narrowed. 'How did you manage to get this one, Macy?'

'Miss Kirby . . .'

'Miss Kirby. Hmm. Were you just about to clap a hand over your beautiful mouth, my sweet?'

Oh, God! It was getting too involved. Feeling sweat trickling down her back, Macy tried to avoid her husband's probing glance. 'Wendy's her niece . . .'

Brice paused as his quick mind grappled with such intelligence. 'When Miss Kirby mentioned that her niece needed an assistant, did you say you would do it to pass the time or because you were short of money?'

Macy's scarlet cheeks mercifully saved her from having to give an answer which might have infuriated Brice even more than the slightly wrong conclusions he immediately jumped to.

'My God!' he breathed. 'I can only hope that Miss Kirby used what brains she is blessed with! If I thought for a moment that she'd believed you, I think I might kill you!'

Her voice cracked. 'You keep threatening . . .'

'If we don't get out of here,' he grated, 'I'll do more than that. Get your coat, Macy, before I begin following threats with actions!'

There followed a period of relative calm. Macy felt depressed over her lost job but Brice's attitude discouraged her from trying to find another. His fury over what he termed her blatant deceit eventually disappeared but his renewed distrust of her never did. He took to ringing her at odd hours and even occasionally arrived unexpectedly at Kate's to check she was there. When Kate and Miss Kirby teased her about her adoring husband, she would have liked to have believed them but she knew in her heart it was far from the truth.

Nevertheless, when her aunt died, he proved a tower of strength. It happened suddenly. Late one evening, as they were thinking of going to bed, the phone rang and when Brice returned from answering it, compassion had replaced the look of desire in his eyes.

'That was Miss Kirby,' he said gently. 'Kate's very ill, Macy.'

Minutes later, they were on their way. Knowing it was useless at this stage trying to help her, Brice explained that Kate had gone into a coma half an hour ago, and when Macy said tearfully that she should have been there, he retorted sharply that she had done all she could. 'You gave her your love and attention in abundance, Macy. You won't help her by reproaching yourself now. If you do, she could sense it and, if it is time ...' he put a comforting hand over hers, 'it might only distress her.'

Macy nodded numbly while her fingers curled convulsively round his.

'Try and be brave, for Kate's sake,' he added softly.

The doctor had arrived before them but Kate only opened her eyes once. It was, as Brice said, as though she knew they were there and she smiled faintly but happily at the sight of Macy standing in the circle of her husband's arm.

'She was content,' Brice murmured as they withdrew to the kitchen afterwards and Miss Kirby assured Macy that her aunt had been content ever since she had got married.

The days seemed to drag for a long time after the funeral. Macy realised she was missing Kate and although she knew the worst of her sadness would eventually pass, she didn't know what she was going to put in Kate's place. For a while her time had been filled with her job at the florists and keeping her aunt company. Now that this had been taken away, the days were curiously empty.

May brought a spell of really fine weather, and perhaps because she looked so pale and strained, Brice took her to the country for a day.

'I was born here and have been back occasionally,' he said. 'But I'm in no way familiar with the countryside outside your cities. You can spend Sunday showing me something of it, if you like. It will put some colour in your cheeks and do me good to get right away from the office.'

Macy knew what he meant. He didn't usually go to the factory at weekends but he brought work home to be pursued in his study. 'You won't see much in one day,' she warned him dryly.

'Next month I'll take a long weekend,' he promised, 'and we'll go further. I'd like to see your English Lakes and Scotland but the border counties might do for a start.'

As they set out, Macy thought pensively—it's never our city or country, he talks as though he's a visitor. She never asked if he had reached a decision over returning to the States. She would know soon enough and she hadn't the courage to precipitate a decision that was unlikely to include her. Though he made love to her, she realised he didn't love her and the hope which had once been fresh in her heart was slowly dying.

Nevertheless, he had been kind when her aunt had died. Macy wasn't sure how she would have got through everything without him. And this trip today surely proved he was still trying to be kind, despite the distrust of her that continued to plague him. Maybe in time, she prayed, as she did so frequently, he will learn to love and trust me?

He took the road that by-passed Rochdale, Whitworth and went through Bacup, a town in the Irwell valley, surrounded by stretches of moorland close to the Yorkshire border.

CAPTIVE OF FATE 135

Macy felt her spirits rising as they travelled on quieter roads through the ancient forest of Rossendale. Lowering the car window slightly, she sniffed at the pure country air and said how good it felt to be out.

'You've been too pale lately.' Brice shot her a frowning glance. 'I realise you're missing your aunt but you still shouldn't look as pale as you do.'

Macy hadn't been feeling so good but she didn't mention this to Brice. She had a good idea what was wrong with her but she wasn't ready to do anything about it yet. Since Kate had died there had been a kind of silent truce between them. He didn't watch her as closely and wasn't so critical. She wanted it to stay this way and if what she suspected was true, Brice wasn't going to like it.

The valleys were green and there were signs of spring everywhere, even in less sheltered places. Macy's spirits continued to soar as they parked the car on the wild Cliviger moors and walked over the lonely fells to find the spot where she wanted to picnic. Brice slung the rucksack containing their lunch on his back. He had told Mrs Bland to put in only flasks and sandwiches that could be carried easily.

Macy was surprised to see how good he looked in jeans and a thin shirt with a pullover knotted carelessly over his broad shoulders. She was used to seeing him in business suits and how he was dressed this morning revealed his masculinity in a way she found devastating.

She didn't realise she was staring until she saw his raised brows and the excuse she produced was less than convincing. 'I was thinking, with our unpredictable weather you should maybe have brought a waterproof rather than a pullover?'

'We can't always be worrying over the next bad spell,' he shrugged, and she wondered if it was just the weather he was alluding to.

Brice walked swiftly, his long strides covering the ground so rapidly it took Macy all her time to keep up.

Before they reached the place by a stream she was looking for she was curiously exhausted and glad to stop.

The sight of some clumps of wild flowers revived her though. 'Oh, look!' she cried, as Brice lowered his rucksack to the ground with a grunt. 'Aren't they beautiful!'

'Yes,' he agreed, but his eyes were fixed on her suddenly animated face. 'You haven't smiled much lately, have you?'

Kneeling by the small yellow blooms, she caressed a petal reverently with a long slender finger. 'I suppose not.'

'I know not,' he retorted grimly.

She sighed, her oval face dreamy, speaking almost to herself, 'I wish I could draw again...'

'No!'

Macy glanced up, startled, to find his face nearly as black as the one small cloud creeping over the horizon. Unhappily, she wished she had held her tongue. He had been in such a good mood, now she had spoiled it!

Attempting to restore his former indulgence, she said quickly, 'Don't take any notice—it was just wishful thinking.'

Cool grey eyes were trained on her, eyes that revealed he was far from impressed. 'Don't pretend, Macy. I can read you like a book. All the time you're itching to start designing again. God knows what you get up to when my back's turned.'

Her face whitened under his unexpected attack yet she knew a defensive urge to stick to her guns. 'I've been thinking, Brice,' she looked at him eagerly, 'I could start a small business of my own, working from home. Northholt is so big I could work there without disturbing anyone. There's always a demand for, say, individually designed teatowels...'

'Are you mad?' he rasped harshly, not sparing her. 'You could never hope to succeed. You lack a most essential thing. Integrity.'

She was beyond feeling hurt. 'It doesn't seem so essential today,' she retorted dryly. 'And how could I deceive anyone with a few teatowels?'

'You'd find a way,' he bit back cynically.

'So . . .' she cried bitterly, 'if I have talent, because of one mistake I'm to be condemned to wasting it. Oh,' she swallowed painfully, 'I'm not proud of what I did but surely you have to forgive me sometime?'

'I set no time limit.'

He hadn't. Brushing back wisps of hair from off her hot forehead, she sat down bleakly in the rough fell grass. All about them the high moors stretched, even in greener places wild and lonely, interspersed by the dry stone walls that farmers cared for so meticulously and sheep and the weather so frequently damaged. And people occasionally! Macy loved it here but she knew she could put roots down anywhere with Brice. Her real attachment was to him, not to one particular place or country. Yet he despised her. The only place she was tempted to believe she was really necessary to him was in bed. There his passion for her remained unabated, but knowing how compatible they were often brought more fear than comfort. If nothing changed between them, could she live with him forever, in the shadow of his distrust? How long would he allow her to? He must know many beautiful women. How long before he sought to impart on one of them the love and companionship he denied his wife?

Brice stood staring into the distance, his mouth compressed, then with a sigh he dropped down beside her and opened the rucksack. Silently he passed her a flask, retaining one for himself. 'I told Mrs Bland not to pack much,' he said. 'I don't mind a feast on the beach but I don't think it's advisable for a day's hiking. We can stuff ourselves this evening.'

Macy chewed a sandwich slowly, until it stopped threatening to choke her. If he could make an effort so must she. 'What's this like compared with the States, Brice?'

He seemed to appreciate her co-operation for his face briefly softened. 'You can't compare the two places, Macy. The difference in size alone makes it impossible, yet I sometimes think distances in the States can be conquered more easily than here. Over there, in most cities, you can step on a fast jet and be anywhere in practically an hour or two. Whereas here, even getting to an airport can take twice that time.'

'Surely you aren't criticising our transport facilities?' she teased.

He grinned back, a little relief of some kind in the grey eyes. 'A guest should never criticise what a host provides.'

With a hand that wasn't quite steady she poured coffee into her flask top. 'So you might not stay?'

'I still haven't reached a decision, Macy. Nothing can be done in a hurry but once the business is on its feet again, there might be no further need here for my particular talents. I may put a manager in, there's plenty excellent ones going a-begging, and liaise between here and the States.'

None of his plans seemed to include her. Determined not to dwell on it, she said brightly. 'Alec would have been proud of you. You've done wonders already.'

'I would like to think he is,' Brice replied gently. 'The business was run down but Alec was getting on and a single man of his age can lose interest. If he'd ever given any indication that he needed help I would have come over and given it to him, free, gratis.'

Somehow Macy didn't doubt it. And with Brice's brilliant reputation well known, she could imagine the difference it would have made. She nodded, saying slowly, 'I never heard of him being unhappy.'

Brice smiled. 'I'm sure he wasn't, and he probably didn't feel like being shaken up anyway.'

Suspecting the truth of this from what she'd heard, Macy marvelled at his astuteness, but the sun was warm and she was sleepily disinclined to ponder too deeply.

'That was good,' she said, stifling a yawn and stirring herself to repack the remains of their meal.

'By rights,' Brice quipped, sounding equally lazy, 'we should now stretch out on a rug and make love. Can you imagine it?'

She could and shivered. She couldn't imagine anything more sensuous than lying naked in Brice's arms in the soft grass by the stream and afterwards reviving their exhausted bodies in the cool, sparkling water. As her flushed cheeks betrayed her, she knew, despite his mocking tones that he was tempted when he drew her almost roughly to her feet and pulled her against him. She felt the hardness of his body and gasped at the raw desire in the kiss he pressed fiercely on her quivering lips, but before she could respond he had thrust her away again and was stooping to pick up the rucksack.

They walked for the rest of the afternoon, returning to the car about six and arriving home tired but relaxed to share the meal Mrs Bland had left for them in the oven. They showered first but were both so hungry after their light lunch and a day spent in the open that they didn't linger. Later, replete, they loaded the dishwasher and retired to the lounge to have their coffee in front of a blazing log fire.

Brice had put a match to the fire for the evening had grown cool. Now, as they sat cosily before it, he swirled the brandy in his glass and glanced at Macy thoughtfully. 'You've never told me anything about your parents, Macy. Perhaps,' he admitted wryly, 'because I never asked.'

She had been looking at him. He so seldom spent an hour with her like this and she found it difficult to take her eyes off him. Now she looked away. She wasn't sure whether she wanted to discuss her parents, yet his manner was so relaxed that she didn't want to risk spoiling it again, as she had done that afternoon.

'I can't remember my mother,' she replied slowly. 'She died when I was born. That was when Kate came to live with us. I think by doing that she must have sacrificed any chance of having a family of her own. Not only that, as soon as I was old enough for school, she returned to being a secretary again, just to keep the house going.'

'Where was your father?' Brice frowned. 'I gather he was still around?'

'Yes,' Macy's soft mouth twisted slightly. 'He died only two years ago. After he left university I believe he was convinced he could make a living writing, but he never did. But for Aunt Kate, I think we might have starved.'

Brice's voice hardened. 'Didn't he realise he had responsibilities?'

'That was the trouble,' Macy sighed. 'He never took anything seriously except his writing. He said life was never meant to be a continual struggle.'

'But he obviously didn't mind how hard anyone else struggled,' Brice intervened dryly.

Macy was ashamed that she felt no surge of loyalty but she remained silent. 'Anyway,' she said at last, 'Kate put me through art school and everything. She did such a lot, which I realised, when I grew up, must have been a terrible strain yet I never heard her grumble.'

Brice said cynically. 'The world will always be peopled by those who give and those who take, my sweet.'

Macy mulled over this. Which category did he put her in she wondered. As though sensing her reluctance to talk of her father, he asked no more questions and she offered nothing further. What was the use, she thought despondently. Brice could have no permanent interest in either her or her family.

At last he stirred and stretched. 'Your English air has proved too much for me,' he grinned. 'How about an early night? I could do with a bath as well, otherwise I might be as stiff as a board in the morning.'

She couldn't believe it. A more superb physical specimen than Brice, she didn't think she was likely to meet. Since coming home he had pulled on a pair of dark trousers and a sweater which outlined his powerful body in a way that increased her heartbeats as rapidly as his jeans had done. As her pulse began throbbing heavily again, she forced herself to retort dryly, 'If anyone's going to be stiff it must be me. I could scarcely keep up with you today.'

His brows quirked as his eyes roamed over her, as though she'd provided him with a legitimate excuse. When she moved uneasily under such close surveillance and restively tossed back her long dark hair, he noticed how it gleamed with iridescent blue lights and looked almost too heavy for the slenderness of her neck.

'You're an agile little girl, all the same,' he laughed, with a hint of superior male condescension. 'Beautiful, as well,' his voice deepened slightly, 'I had to walk in front of you, otherwise my eyes wouldn't have been concentrated on the view. I wasn't trying to prove superiority.'

She flushed, her hands going unconsciously to her waist. 'I'm not putting on weight, am I?'

'That wasn't what I meant,' he retorted, 'and you know it. You've always been too sexy for my peace of mind.'

With a smile, he rose, holding out his hand. Her heart thumping, she put hers into it and went upstairs with him. So much electricity vibrated between them that Macy could hardly retain her composure yet she waited quietly while he filled the bath and betrayed no visible sign that she was inwardly trembling as he undressed her. What was the use of struggling against either Brice or herself? she thought resignedly. Brice might not like her but he took every advantage of what she had to offer. Yet she couldn't accuse him of being selfish—he usually made sure she received as much pleasure as she gave. And when they were like this they seemed to dissolve into a single unity, becoming one, not two persons. In his arms she lost all sense of reality and responded, she suspected, exactly as he intended her to.

This evening he kissed her passionately, a shudder of sexual excitement rippling through his entire body as they lay together in the warm caressing water. Moaning deep in her throat, Macy slid her arms round him, conscious of the tips of her breasts brushing his chest and her slender limbs being crushed by the bones and sheer muscle of his. His kisses became deep and hungry and her response just as primitive as heated blood surged through her veins. When later he lifted her out of the bath she was aware of nothing but the raw desire they shared as he carried her to the bedroom.

The following morning, Macy went to see her doctor who confirmed the suspicions she had been harbouring for some time. For all she was half-prepared she still felt quite stunned when she was informed she was pregnant. Numbly she caught a bus into the city, unable to face the rest of the day alone at Northholt wondering how to break the news to Brice when he returned home that evening.

Suddenly she decided to go to the factory to ask him to take her out for lunch. He had told her not to go to the factory but surely he would forgive her when he heard what she had to tell him. Now that the first shock had worn off, she felt thrilled about the baby and wanted him to share her excitement. She was in the lift on her way to his office, when she realised he might not feel as pleased as she was, but she resolutely thrust the niggling doubts of previous weeks from her. Even if Brice didn't love her, surely he wouldn't find it so difficult to love a son or daughter?

As she left the lift there was someone waiting to go

CAPTIVE OF FATE 143

down in it and to her surprise she saw it was her old supervisor, George Paley.

'Macy!' he exclaimed, a smile spreading across his kindly face when he caught sight of her. 'Sorry,' he apologised, ruefully, 'I should have said, Mrs Sinclair.'

'Macy will do,' she smiled back at him tentatively, delighted to see him but apprehensive of Brice's reactions if he discovered who she had met. He hadn't been pleased about Tim Matthews and although it didn't seem possible that he could accuse her of having a love affair with George Paley, he might still be angry.

George Paley laughed teasingly. 'I must confess your marriage surprised me, Macy, but I'm glad of the opportunity to wish you every happiness. I've already congratulated your husband and told him how everyone considers him a lucky fellow.'

After Macy thanked him, without saying that she doubted that Brice shared his opinion, he added, 'It was a bit of a setback for me losing both you and Thelma in the same week. I suppose you know Thelma's gone to South Africa. She's been writing to a few of us and seems very happy.'

As George hurried off, Macy continued on her way to Brice's office. Why, she wondered, should Thelma be writing to anyone? She had never been that friendly with the staff in the department, having always considered herself superior to her work-mates. Macy gulped but refused to believe that Thelma could be out to make mischief. The brief glimpse of something she had caught in George Paley's eyes, when he first saw her, couldn't mean a thing? And wasn't Thelma too far away to be able to make trouble now?

If Macy had thought it unfortunate that she should bump into George, when she found Tim Matthews in Brice's outer office talking to Miss Drake, she wished she had followed her intuition, however belatedly, and stayed away.

Miss Drake appeared as surprised as George had

been to see her but as she and Tim turned simultaneously as Macy knocked briefly on the open door, her startled glance was swiftly disguised by a welcoming smile.

'Why, good morning, Mrs Sinclair,' she murmured smoothly. 'What can I do for you?'

Macy smiled nervously, trying to avoid looking at Tim. 'I called to see my husband...'

'Oh, what a shame!' Miss Drake exclaimed, 'I'm afraid he isn't in. He's taken Miss Claremont, you remember the head of Claremont Boutiques, out for lunch, and they left early.'

Macy felt a faint flush steal into her pale cheeks. 'I should have phoned beforehand,' she murmured awkwardly.

'Was it anything important?' Miss Drake asked, clearly doing her best to be helpful.

Macy avoided a direct answer. 'I was in town,' she had been going to say shopping until she remembered she wasn't carrying anything. 'I was just going to ask Brice to drive me home.'

'Oh, dear,' Miss Drake frowned, before her face lit up with a flash of inspiration as she turned to Tim. 'Why not let Mr Matthews take you. I'm sure Mr Sinclair would approve.'

Tim's eyes met Macy's, both blank with consternation. He hadn't spoken so far, she realised, for he was obviously as embarrassed as she was. However, he answered Miss Drake with more presence of mind than Macy would have given him credit for.

'I've that meeting in a few minutes, Miss Drake, which you know I daren't miss, but I'm sure if I can't run Mrs Sinclair home myself, I'll have time to arrange for someone else to give her a lift.'

A moment later Macy found herself outside with Tim's gasp of relief ringing in her ears. Not liking to make her own relief so obvious, she murmured, 'Thanks, Tim. We can't blame Miss Drake for making the wrong suggestion and, anyway, I can find my own way home. I've really nothing better to do.'

Tim sighed rather savagely. 'If you were anyone but the boss's wife, Macy, I wouldn't give a damn, but he's just coming round from the last time.'

'I was sorry about that,' Macy stammered, 'I tried to explain . . .'

'It's not your fault for having a jealous husband,' Tim grimaced wryly, 'but if it happens again I can kiss good bye to any chances of promotion. Much as I love you, darling, I can't afford to risk offending him again.'

'You aren't exactly a knight on a white charger, are you, Tim?' Macy couldn't help giggling as he kept glancing furtively over his shoulder, as if expecting Brice to appear any minute.

'It's a wise man who knows when he's beaten,' Tim replied reproachfully, kissing her quickly on the cheek, to refute any notion that he was a coward.

Macy didn't feel so good by the time she got home. Having refused to let Tim call her a taxi, she had struggled home in the heat. Normally, catching a hundred buses mightn't have bothered her and she blamed her feeling of exhaustion on her reactions to the morning's events. Listlessly she pushed the lunch Mrs Bland insisted on making for her around on her plate, unable to stop picturing Brice having his with the beautiful Miss Claremont!

Carrying her coffee upstairs, she decided to lie down for an hour. She still felt unwell and suddenly she didn't want to take any risks with the precious new life she was carrying.

Removing her thin cotton dress, she took a good, if disinterested look at herself. Three months pregnant, Dr Hutton had said. She was amazed to find she was still as slim as ever. That would soon change, though. She studied her figure ruefully. She was used to being very slender. How would she feel when her clothes wouldn't fit? Perhaps, more important, how would

Brice feel? Would he begin comparing her expanding proportions with women like Miss Claremont?

With an impatient sigh that she couldn't get the other woman completely out of her mind, Macy glanced at her hair. It needed cutting. It was as thick and shining as ever but a few inches off the ends would help. Frowning, she noticed how the sun had caught her fair skin yesterday on the moors, but as she had no money for either a hair cut or sun-screen oil, there was nothing she could do about it. Never mind, she comforted herself, lovingly patting her stomach, now she had something money couldn't buy—and infinitely more precious.

She must have slept far longer than she intended for she woke with a start to find Brice standing over her.

'What time is it?' she asked, her sapphire blue eyes wide with dismay. She had hoped to be bathed and dressed before he came home. She had planned to be poised and pretty when she told him her news, not hot and untidy as she was now.

'After six,' he snapped.

'Oh,' she gasped, scarcely able to believe it. 'I only meant to rest for an hour. I must have been tired.'

'Exhausted!' he jeered contemptuously. 'After spending the afternoon with Matthews.'

Turning from him convulsively, Macy hid her shocked face in her hands. How did he know she had seen Tim? Miss Drake, of course, would have mentioned it. 'I didn't spend the afternoon with him,' she muttered, making an effort to pull herself together and look at him again while despairing that everything was going so wrong.

'You came to the factory,' Brice retorted bitingly, 'when I specifically asked you not to, so how do I know you aren't seeing Matthews behind my back?'

Silently she shook her head. 'I know what you said,' she whispered. 'And I had no intention of disobeying you, but as I was in town I thought it might be nice to come and see you. I was going to ask you to take me for lunch.'

'I had already made arrangements with another beautiful lady,' he taunted unfeelingly.

Pain lanced through Macy's heart. 'I know,' she said tonelessly. 'Miss Drake informed me.'

'It was business,' he muttered, as if against his will.

'Nice for Miss Claremont, all the same,' Macy retorted stormily.

'At least I had some excuse,' he flung back. 'You had none for blatantly making assignations with your boyfriend in my office.'

Macy drew a ragged breath. 'I didn't do that. And it was Miss Drake who suggested that Tim should see me home but I caught the bus.'

'I wish I could believe it,' he exclaimed, grey eyes icy.

Suddenly his distrust of her shattered her mind and she cried without meaning to, 'You think I'd go out with another man when I'm expecting your child?' Brice might have been shot, judging from the shock on his face. He went quite pale, tension making a white ring round his tight mouth. 'God!' he muttered, 'You're sure . . .?'

As pale as he was, Macy stared back at him. Could she have made a greater mess of things? It would have been easy to have told him gently instead of bursting out like that! Nevertheless, she said stoutly, 'It's not something I'd pretend about.'

'You wouldn't be the first,' he retorted tightly.

Numbly she retaliated. 'You may be speaking from experience but it's never happened to me before. And if you won't take my word for it, you can always ring my doctor.'

'That won't be necessary,' he said stiffly, 'and I'm referring to what's common knowledge, not personal experience. Until now I've never been that careless.'

'Then you can't be surprised,' she murmured hollowly.

'I suppose not,' he allowed mockingly, 'seeing what you're like in bed. But it rather complicates matters, doesn't it?'

What did he mean? No doubt he didn't like the idea of her bearing his offspring. 'I may not pass on my less admirable traits,' she said bitterly. 'If I do, I'm sure you'll soon iron them out.'

'You're sure I'll be around to do that?' he rejoined grimly.

She went white. 'You're insinuating that I've done this deliberately to keep you tied to me?'

He took a step towards her, then, visibly pulling himself up, he swung to the window. Standing with his back to her, he snapped, 'It would take more than that, but a child can come expensive.'

Macy stared at his broad shoulders which were so often naked above her. She felt completely bewildered and miserable. Her voice cracking under the weight of such misery, she retorted bleakly, 'I'll take full responsibility. You needn't be afraid that I'll sue you for maintenance . . .'

He swung round again, breathing heavily, the fierce glitter in his narrowed eyes overwhelming her. 'How do I know it's mine?' he accused grimly.

CHAPTER NINE

As shock rippled coldly through her, Macy's eyes widened in horror on his. She had a curious feeling that his thoughts were oddly inconsistent with what he was saying but the cruelty of his suspicions brought such pain that she refused to consider he might be fighting something she didn't understand.

'You can't mean that?' she gasped, hot tears beginning to run down her cold cheeks.

Hearing the agony in her voice, a different expression replaced the hard conflict in his eyes and with a sigh of self-repugnance he dropped on the bed beside her, his hands coming out to touch her. 'I'm sorry, Macy.' He ran remorseful fingers over her wet face. He even licked a tear gently off her quivering lips. 'I shouldn't have said that. And don't worry about the baby. I'll look after it.'

If his anger and accusations had terrified her, his sudden sympathy proved too much. What little control she had left disappeared and she began to sob wildly. Burying her face in the side of his neck, she clung to him, letting all her misery wash out, forced to acknowledge that no matter how much he hurt her she still loved and needed him.

'Oh, God, Macy!' He wrapped his arms around her shaking body, enclosing her in an almost painful embrace. 'If only you knew ...!' His groaning words were lost as he began soothing her with tender kisses which, despite the tension between them, soon became a passionate exchange. He kissed her eyes and mouth, smoothing her hair back off her hot forehead and insidiously a new trembling began in Macy that had nothing to do with fear.

With a little moan of surrender she curled her fingers round his neck, parting her lips willingly to the demand of his as exploding shivers of ecstasy trembled over her until she lost all awareness of anything but Brice. The sensuous caresses of his expert hands forever sought to arouse her, moulding her soft body to the muscular contours of his. As his rising desire to possess her became increasingly apparent, Macy soon lost any desire to resist.

Later, as they lay entangled in each others arms, he murmured, 'It's never been as good with anyone else.'

Macy stiffened. What was between them was very powerful but was sex all that attracted him to her?

'How about another run in the country,' he suggested softly, his mouth moving warmly on her smooth skin, sending fresh shivers of rapture along her spine. 'I've heard of a place where we can have dinner.'

Knowing he was trying to please her, she nodded and forgave him the doubts that forever prevailed in him. It wasn't easy to forget his continual distrust but at least he still stayed with her.

As she lay close beside him, he didn't mention the baby again and she decided to give him time to get used to the idea of being a father. Feeling a resurgence of desire stirring in both of them, she sighed that they could want each other so often.

His sigh echoed hers. 'If we stay here, my sweet, there's only one way this can finish up, and I did plan to take you out.' Reluctantly he rolled away from her. 'Stay right where you are,' he commanded mysteriously, 'I won't be a minute.'

Recalling the last time he had said much the same thing, when he had gone to investigate her car, Macy waited, rather apprehensively, until he returned. She didn't allow herself to ponder on his reactions to the baby while he was away, for fear her still precarious control slipped.

He was back much sooner than he had been on the

previous occasion, this time carrying a large oblong box, with the name of the most expensive shop in town emblazoned across it in gold letters.

Placing the box in her arms, he said lightly, 'After I got rid of Miss Claremont this afternoon, I went shopping for this. I hope it fits.'

Macy's small face lit with pleasure. She couldn't remember receiving such an interesting looking present before and it was the first one Brice had given her. Smoothing the silver wrappings with her fingers, she gazed down on it in considerable awe.

'Aren't you going to open it?' Brice asked, quite patiently for him.

Flushing a little, she eagerly tore off the wrappings and removed the lid. Scrambling to her feet, at this point, she lifted a self-spotted silk dress in fresh sugar crystal shades from its bed of white tissue. It had soft puffed sleeves and an easy summery line that would not only fit but suit her. There were high-heeled sandals to match as well as a pale silky shawl. Macy wouldn't have liked to have tried to guess how much it had cost!

'It's beautiful!' she breathed, touching it reverently. 'I'm almost scared to wear it...'

'I bought it for you to wear tonight,' Brice said sternly. 'I spent a lot of time choosing it and I'd like to be rewarded for my trouble.'

Macy smiled as she thanked him, impulsively kissing his hard cheek. She could imagine how Miss Drake had frowned on him disapprovingly as he'd returned to the office, believing he had spent the whole afternoon with Miss Claremont.

She hung the dress up while she showered and made up her face. Brice, quicker than she was, sat on the end of the bed watching as she completed her toilet. She brushed her hair until it shone then applied a little lip gloss to her slightly swollen lips and mascara to emphasise her already enormous eyes. When she was finished, with her dress on and neatly belted to her still narrow waist, she knew she looked good by the kind of stunned appreciation on Brice's face as he stared at her.

A little colour crept to her own face as she studied him briefly in return. He was tall and big but more elegant than any other man she had seen. His features were strong with his mouth and chin determined and she noted his wide shoulders and almost animal litheness that even faultlessly tailored clothes couldn't hide.

With a mocking grin, maybe in silent acknowledgment of the mutual admiration they were exchanging, he picked up her shawl and dropped it around her shoulders. Not until then did he appear to notice the faint redness on her thin arms.

'What happened?' he frowned, touching the tender skin carefully.

'I got sunburned yesterday,' she answered lightly. 'But it's stopped hurting now.'

'There are plenty of good sunscreens on the market,' he said tersely. 'For goodness sake get yourself some tomorrow.'

'I can't,' she shrugged, decided she may as well be frank, 'I haven't any money.'

For a moment he stared at her, his good mood evaporating. 'You should have reminded me,' he said stiffly.

He hadn't needed reminding, Macy felt sure. He wasn't a mean man but for some perverse reason it suited him to keep her short of money. Unevenly she sighed. 'If you won't let me earn anything, I have to rely on you for everything but don't let's quarrel again, this evening.'

It must have been the right approach for after drawing a deep breath, he relaxed behind quirking brows. 'You're right, of course, why spoil a pleasant evening by falling out over money? From now on you'll receive an allowance.' Tenderly he touched her arm again, 'We can't risk anything worse happening to your beautiful skin.'

Brice had chosen a pleasant hotel set in its own grounds a few miles from the city. A business acquaintance had recommended it, he said, when Macy asked how he'd known about it. She should have enjoyed it for the food was delicious and the service impeccable. It was understandable, she supposed, that after Brice's discouraging response about the baby that she should still be feeling rather tense, but she was sure she had something else on her mind.

It wasn't until they were on their way home that she remembered what it was. Feeling compelled to mention it, for fear it might have repercussions on Brice's business, she confessed nervously.

'You won't like this, Brice, but I bumped into George Paley, today, and he told me that Thelma Brown has been writing to several people in the department.'

Brice didn't reply for a few seconds, when he did his voice was tight. 'It's possible—but did you have to tell me about it, Macy? I was trying to forget that particular episode.'

But never quite succeeding, her heart cried, while she retorted wearily, 'So am I, but I thought I should pass on what George said.'

'Why?'

'That's just it,' Macy answered helplessly. 'I'm not sure.'

'You're frightened she can do you some harm?'

'That she could do you—the firm some harm.'

'I don't think so,' he retorted, glancing swiftly to her pale bent head and clenched hands. 'No one made Miss Brown leave us, Macy. I may have said one or two things that set her thinking but she was never threatened or blackmailed in any way. I don't believe we have anything to fear.'

Macy tried to take comfort from this and put Thelma out of her mind, and during the days and weeks that followed she thought she had succeeded. Thelma couldn't do her any harm, she would agree, but she was

Brice's wife now and this was difficult enough for him. It wouldn't help him to have rumours circulating about her. When she heard nothing more, however, she was inclined to agree with him that they had nothing to fear.

Each week now, he made her an allowance though he liked to know how she spent it. When he learned she was just using half of it, he gave her less and said he would put the rest away for her. Again she was convinced he wasn't motivated by meanness but when she protested that she was quite capable of saving it herself, this didn't appear to suit him. Clearly he didn't like the idea of her having a nest-egg, and, while Macy had no desire for one herself, she couldn't help wondering why?

When she sold her car for two hundred pounds, she nearly offered the money to him to go towards what she felt she owed him, but deciding he might only scorn such a small repayment, she put it safely away until she could add to it. It was the gardener who asked if she would sell the car to his son and somehow the deal was completed without Brice being any the wiser. If Brice didn't want the money, she thought it would be nice to be able to buy something for the baby when it arrived.

Brice never talked about the baby so she still had no means of knowing exactly how he felt about it. She fretted over this but forced herself to be content with the extra care he gave her. Otherwise, apart from still liking to cuddle her close in bed, his general demeanour towards her grew more and more distant. Sometimes she wondered if she was supposed to notice the reviving cups of tea he brought her when early morning sickness plagued her for a while—or that he took her shopping at weekends so that he could carry any parcels for her. She felt pampered in a totally impersonal way and oddly helpless to change the kind of life she was leading. Mrs Bland did the cooking and housekeeping, a man did the garden, and a cleaning firm dealt with all the rough work. Macy felt it might have been easier to find a needle in a haystack than a job to occupy herself with!

When Mrs Bland left to spend her annual holiday with her sister, Macy almost danced for joy. She was careful to hide her jubilation, of course, as Mrs Bland wished her a very reluctant goodbye. Macy was certain that, had it not been for her sister's persistence, Mrs Bland would never have gone.

'I'm looking forward to the next two weeks,' she smiled at Brice when he came home that night. Her face, which had grown too thin and pale lately, glowed as he turned to look at her, eyebrows raised. 'Mrs Bland will be away but you won't miss her. I'm quite a good cook. You'll see,' she added, not so confidently, as his face darkened.

'I don't wish to—see,' he drawled coldly. 'While I don't doubt your prowess as a cook, I've already arranged for someone to take over Mrs Bland's duties until she returns.'

Macy refused to believe it. She went degrees paler but looked back at him with more defiance than she had shown for some time. 'Then you'll just have to tell, whoever it is you've made arrangements with, that I intend managing myself.'

'I'll do no such thing.' The grey of his eyes went black with anger. 'You have to understand, Macy. I must run my life as though you weren't here.'

Glaring at him in a small fury, Macy jumped to her feet. 'How can you pretend I'm not here?' she spluttered inconsistently. 'For one thing there's too much of me . . .'

'You can't blame me entirely for that!' he retorted icily, a pulse beating warningly in his jaw as he stared insolently down on her swelling stomach.

'Blame you!' she cried hysterically, feeling incredibly wounded. 'I don't blame either of us. Blame isn't a word I associate with my baby . . .!'

'You're hysterical,' Brice snapped, 'God help me if the child takes after you.'

She had to calm down. She had been told to relax the last time she attended the clinic. Several men had been there with their wives but Brice hadn't numbered among them. She was healthy physically, the doctor had said, but a little too tense. She knew he believed she was nervous about having the baby and she let him think this, rather than have him suspect there was anything wrong with her marriage.

She looked at Brice bitterly. 'Whether it's a boy or girl,' she retorted fiercely, 'I hope they learn the art of forgiveness!'

The next morning, Brice left home so early she didn't see him. There was no cup of tea by her bedside and he hadn't slept with her that night. It was the first time they hadn't shared a bed since they were married and she had woken several times in the night with his name on her lips. She missed him so much that only pride and tears prevented her from going and seeing where he was and what he was doing. And she couldn't forget what he'd said about having to live his life as if she wasn't there. It seemed more than a hint that sometime in the future he intended getting rid of her.

The new woman had arrived when she got downstairs and was every bit as reserved and efficient as Mrs Bland. Macy didn't have to advise her on anything as she appeared to know everything. She waited hopefully to be consulted but she never was. Miss Gregory seemed to know where everything was kept and found her way about the house so easily that Macy suspected that either Brice had shown her over earlier, or that Mrs Bland had invited her in while Macy was out.

In an attempt to get rid of the feeling that she was superfluous, Macy climbed to one of the attics after lunch, deciding to sort out the things she had salvaged and stored when Kate's home had been sold up. There was nothing of any value, for the few antiques they'd had they had parted with when money had become scarce with Kate's illness. Poking around, Macy paused when she saw her paints, then impulsively ran back downstairs to the garden, to gather a small bunch of flowers. Returning to the attic, she began painting and, to her delight, found the old magic still flowed through her fingers on to the canvas.

The light in the attic wasn't good but an hour was all she needed to be sure she could still capture the exact likeness of the flowers as beautifully as she used to do. From this she derived the reassurance she realised she had been unconsciously seeking. It was comforting to know that if Brice didn't want her any more, she would be capable of at least earning a living without having to depend either on alimony or charity.

When Brice arrived home at his usual time she was surprised and even more so when, like a small boy, he drew from behind his back a bunch of exotic hothouse flowers. As she flushed, because the flowers reminded her guiltily of what she'd been doing, he put them warily into her arms.

'For me?' she breathed, her lovely eyes suddenly radiant as she buried her face in the sweet smelling blooms.

'For you,' he said gravely, his glance fixed on her bent head, the pure, child-like nape revealed by the thick pony-tail and the delicate curve of her cheek. 'I thought you might like them,' he added huskily.

This was another way of saying he was sorry and his words were like music in Macy's ears. She daren't do more than nod in case she spoiled things by bursting into tears.

Brice cleared his throat and dug his hands in his pockets. 'How would you feel about going to a party, this evening?' he asked carefully. 'You're looking better and it might not do you any harm to get out a bit. We haven't been far lately.'

Whose fault was that? Macy glanced at him quickly but didn't speak her thoughts aloud. Any harmony between them was too precious to spoil with careless words. 'If you don't mind being seen with a very pregnant lady,' she teased softly, 'I have that very attractive maternity dress you bought me.'

He laughed, the hard tension suddenly easing from his face. 'Come here,' he coaxed, reaching for her, drawing her close, kissing her soft eyelids closed. 'I can help you shower and we'll go after dinner. Did you miss me last night?'

'I did,' Macy confessed, then teased, 'The bed was cold.'

'It won't be cold tonight,' he promised softly as with his arm still around her they went upstairs.

The new maternity gown was a great success. Its voluminous folds and Macy's thinness hid the fact that she was getting near the end of her pregnancy. Because Brice was being kind to her again and paying her compliments, her blue eyes sparkled with happiness. She didn't realise how the curiously young, untouched look about her made her husband swallow and increased his heart-beats.

Macy saw his mouth tighten but ignored the faint chill that swept over her as he helped her carefully into his car. It was in moments like this that he could make her feel she meant something to him. 'What kind of party are we going to?' she asked, wondering why she hadn't asked before.

'One of the directors is having a wedding anniversary,' he replied briefly.

'Won't it be a family affair?' Macy frowned.

'Apparently not.' Brice shrugged. 'He and his wife seem to be always giving parties. She's obviously very sociable and I've refused so many times that I half-promised to come to this one.'

Macy knew of the competition among some of the firm's wives to provide the best entertainment. Having been to some of these parties before, she couldn't say she was terribly enthusiastic. This evening she felt even less so.

'What will I say if anyone asks about our wedding?' she muttered uncertainly.

Brice sighed impatiently. 'Who is going to be asking about that after all these months? And remember, most of the people you'll meet tonight are employed by me. Enid Alston isn't going to be forgetting that. She's a bit of a bitch but she's very ambitious for her husband. She isn't likely to be going to risk him losing his job by plying you with awkward questions.'

'Other people might, though.'

Brice shook his head. 'I doubt it. It's not as if we weren't properly married and people soon forget.'

'I wouldn't wish to spoil your evening,' Macy sighed.

'Don't be foolish,' he retorted curtly. 'You couldn't do that. I wasn't keen in the first place. If you had refused to come, I certainly wouldn't have come by myself.'

Macy believed him when he said this. He shut her out with work—not by socialising without her.

His director's house was almost an hour's drive from Northholt. Macy didn't recognise the district but she could see it was a lot smarter than the area where they lived. The house was smart, too, as were their hosts and most of their guests. She found herself wondering dryly if they had been hand-picked to blend beautifully with the sophisticated surroundings? As far as this went, Brice must be the ultimate goal of every ambitious hostess. Macy couldn't see a man to match him. He was impressive, and she saw several women watching him avidly when they were scarcely inside the door. It had something to do with his charm and vitality but his commanding figure caught the eye immediately.

Enid Alston, their hostess, drew him eagerly to her side and began doing the rounds with him. If Brice hadn't kept such a determined hold on her, Macy would have been lost off in the first few yards. Eventually Mrs Alston paused and began talking about babies. Macy wasn't sure whether she meant to be kind or was drawing attention to her bulging figure. Whatever the woman's reasons, Macy wished she hadn't mentioned the subject for she could feel Brice withdrawing. His arm left Macy's waist and his expression grew aloof. Macy glanced at Mrs Alston almost bitterly. Was she a clever woman or had she just stumbled inadvertently on a way guaranteed to part them?

'Mine are all grown up now,' Mrs Alston gushed, 'but one never forgets the first years. The nappies and sleepless nights, the illness, anxiety. Of course I hear fathers do a lot to help, nowadays. You wouldn't let your wife get up during the night, would you, Mr Sinclair?'

'I certainly wouldn't!' he said, so meaningly that both Macy and Mrs Alston went slightly pink.

'W-where are your children now?' Macy stammered, feeling pity for Mrs Alston though she wasn't sure that she deserved any.

'Scattered all over the world, my dear,' the other woman regained her composure remarkably quickly. 'Well, two of them are. Rosemary, our youngest, is in her father's office. You know Rosemary, Mr Sinclair.'

Brice nodded. 'I have the pleasure.'

'Of course he knows me, Mummy!' a bright voice interrupted. 'We see each other every day, don't we—Brice?'

'Almost,' Brice qualified, but with a tolerant smile.

Mace experienced what she realised was a pang of unjustified jealousy. Rosemary Alston was young and extremely attractive but Brice didn't seem that taken with her.

When her mother introduced her to Macy, Rosemary's china blue eyes flickered over her disparagingly. 'When is the baby due?' she asked coolly.

'Very soon,' Macy replied reluctantly.

'How—nice,' Rosemary said delicately, clearly meaning, how awful! 'I should hate to be in your condition,' she added sweetly, tugging at the silver belt on her gauzy dress as if to emphasise the difference between Macy's waist and her own.

Colour crept into Macy's cheeks again while Mrs Alston pretended to frown on her daughter who took absolutely no notice. Rosemary tucked her arm through Brice's and smiled up at him charmingly. 'Dance with me, darling,' she murmured, 'I'm sure your wife won't mind.'

To Macy's surprise, Brice obliged, leaving her standing with Mrs Alston. She saw the arm Brice put around Rosemary tighten as the girl put both hers around his neck.

'Rosemary's a sweet girl,' Mrs Alston purred complacently, her glance following Macy's, warm with satisfaction. 'She's good at her work and very fond of your husband, as well.'

Macy nearly said something rude but knew it wouldn't help. Mrs Alston clearly thought her daughter as faultless as an angel. She had the look of an angel, too, fair and innocent, but there was nothing angelic, Macy would have bet, in the calculating coldness of those china blue eyes.

Mrs Alston, murmuring sympathetically that Macy looked pale, took herself off to get her some coffee and forgot to come back. And so did Brice. Seeing him disappearing in the direction of the bar with Rosemary still clinging to him, Macy fought down a fresh wave of jealousy. Brice was a man, a very virile one, and while she didn't think he would be unfaithful to her, like many other men with a wife in her condition, he might be tempted to amuse himself a little when a girl like Rosemary came along. Especially when she was obviously half in love with him.

Macy spent the next hour wandering rather listlessly about. She talked to the factory personnel who were here and though they were mostly quite friendly, they had wives with them who wanted to dance. She was beginning to wish she had stayed at home when Brice returned to sit beside her.

'Enjoying yourself?' he smiled.

'Not a lot,' she confessed honestly.

He glanced at her quickly then away again. 'You shouldn't become totally dependent on me,' he said curtly.

'Don't worry,' she said tightly, feeling like hitting him, 'I won't.'

The silence between them was uncomfortable for a moment. From under her thick screen of lashes, Macy saw Brice flexing his jaw, as if trying to relax it. Suddenly he caught her hand, pulling her gently to her feet. 'Come on,' he persuaded, smiling down on her ruefully. 'Let's try and find ourselves some coffee and sandwiches before Mrs Alston pounces again.'

'Are you going to dance again?' Macy asked stiffly as he loaded a tray from the elaborate buffet and carried it to a quiet corner.

'Not unless you want to?' he said firmly.

'No,' she shook her head ruefully, 'I'd rather not.'

He didn't argue but passed her a vol-au-vent. 'Try these,' he smiled, 'they're very good.'

With a laugh she declined. 'I'm too fat as it is.'

'You're too thin,' he returned with a frown, 'I intend having a word with your doctor.'

Macy's heart warmed. There was nothing wrong with her but it was the first time Brice had suggested doing such a thing. Surely it meant that at last he was beginning to take an interest in the baby?

'I've always been thin,' she said. 'Kate used to stuff me with all kinds of things but it never made any difference. She used to say I had so much energy I burned up all my calories.'

'Most young people do,' Brice agreed, 'but you aren't a child any more. And you've someone else to think about now. If I'm going to have a son and heir I'd like to be satisfied that everything is all right with him.'

She answered tautly, 'I'm sure Doctor Hutton would have been in touch with you if he'd thought there was anything wrong. And I go to the clinic regularly.'

'By bus?'

'Yes.'

Brice frowned, as if it had only just occurred to him. 'Next time I'll take you. Please remind me.'

Macy swallowed. He talked as though she was his secretary and he was making a business appointment. Nodding blindly, she looked away from him. Would it always be like this between them? she wondered heavily. Every glimpse of happiness dulled by a feeling of disappointment?

Another couple came to talk to them, saving her from answering, then Rosemary arrived, begging Brice to dance with her again. To Macy's unashamed delight, this time he refused coldly. He stayed by her side for the rest of the evening, which didn't suit Rosemary. A scowl marred her pretty face and Macy wondered if she would ever survive the deadly looks the girl threw at her.

At midnight, when Brice murmured it was time to go, she went upstairs to collect her cloak. Pausing to fasten the rather awkward clasp near the slightly open door of one of the other bedrooms, Macy was startled to hear Rosemary talking. Rosemary had a high, penetrating voice and Macy's eyes widened in dismay as she heard what she was saying.

She was obviously speaking to a friend. 'Brice wanted to dance all night with me, poor pet, but he had to pretend otherwise because of his wife. He had to marry her, of course, for the sake of the business. Nobody quite knows what she did but it's no secret that she was practically thrown out overnight. And that can't happen today without good reason! Some reckon she was ill, but Daddy thinks . . .'

Macy didn't wait to hear what Daddy thought! She fled, feeling sick. Small wonder Brice never learned to trust her with these kind of rumours still flying round. Rosemary was peeved and spiteful that Brice, for some reason, had rejected her, but what she was saying was too near the truth to be dismissed lightly. Had Brice heard? she wondered dismally. It seemed more than likely. It was almost impossible, in a firm like Pearsons, not to know what was going on. Such rumours could only be increasing the distrust he already had of her, making him hate the situation he found himself in. He must feel trapped! Macy shivered, her face white. It took her several minutes to compose herself sufficiently to walk downstairs and smile at Brice as though nothing had happened.

The following day he was late in coming home and when he did he told her he was going to the States.

'There are things that require my attention,' he said, 'and I'd rather go now than nearer when the baby's due.'

Macy glanced at him quickly. 'Will you be gone long?'

'I go tomorrow.' Meeting her anxious eyes, he looked away again, sounding oddly strained, 'I should be back later in the week.'

'It will seem strange without you,' she said.

'I'll only be gone a few days.' He went to pour himself a drink and some of the grimness left his expression as he swallowed it. 'I'm sure you won't miss me that much.'

'Of course not.'

Macy realised she was answering mechanically but she couldn't help it. She had been in a state of agitation since the night before and couldn't get rid of it. Not even when Brice slanted her a crooked smile could she respond to the obvious effort he was making to disperse the tension between them. It took all the control she had not to burst into tears and weep over him She had done too much of that already!

Moving in the direction of the dining room, she

murmured, 'We'd better not keep Mrs Gregory waiting any longer. I'll help you pack after dinner.'

'That won't be necessary,' he replied, but pressed her shoulder lightly, as she sat down on the chair he drew out for her, to indicate he appreciated her gesture. 'I've enough clothes over there to provide me with everything I need.'

Macy knew very little of his actual interests in the States, other than that they were extensive. Once, when she asked he had given her such a negative answer that she had known he suspected her motives. Now she asked tentatively, as much for something to say as anything else, 'Have you a proper home over there?'

'Houses—apartments,' his mouth twisted cynically, 'I wouldn't call any of them a home, except one place, maybe.'

'Where is that?' she prompted.

'Near Los Angeles,' he smiled, in such a way that she knew it meant something to him. 'In the country but right on the coast. You'll have to see it, one day.'

'Yes.' She wasn't sure whether he meant it but he was watching her closely. 'Sometime, I'd love to, if you'll take me?'

'It's a promise,' he said softly.

But one you won't have to keep, she vowed silently, making up her mind, quite suddenly, that she must leave him.

The room where she lived in London was small. It had been barely adequate for her own needs and with a baby it was almost impossible. Macy had rented the room for six weeks. Two before the baby was born, one, while she'd been in hospital, three after. She had been lucky to have found any accommodation at all. By sheer coincidence she had overheard two maids talking in the small hotel she had booked into when she had first arrived here. One of them had remarked that her mother had a room vacant as one of her tenants had 'skedaddled' during the night! After making enquiries, Macy had managed to get it, she still wasn't sure how. Perhaps because, after her landlady's unfortunate experience, she was able to pay in advance. The rent wasn't exorbitant and in this aspect, too, she considered herself lucky, for the few hundred pounds she had managed to save might barely be enough to see her through until she began earning again.

The weeks before the baby was born, Macy had collected the material for the fancy table linen she was designing. She found the work absorbing and hoped it would sell. Two large stores which she had approached were definitely interested.

The baby was sleeping. On the whole he was very good. Given to short bursts of temper when he couldn't have his own way but consenting to be good for long periods when he had it. So far he was only concerned with his comfort and food but when he grew up, she suspected, he might have the same touch of arrogance that was evident in his father.

Resolutely she tried not to think of Brice. She had left a note for him, telling him she was going away and not coming back. Mrs Gregory had promised to see he got it. She hadn't said where she was going but he obviously hadn't tried to find her. There had been no hint of a search anywhere. He must have realised, as she had, that their marriage wasn't going to work and was better finished.

CHAPTER TEN

THERE came a knock on the door and although Macy laid her work aside she hesitated to answer it. The house was large, a rabbit-warren of small rooms. Her landlady didn't live on the premises and lately small boys had been amusing themselves by pestering the residents.

Hating to let any heat escape when it was so expensive, she opened the door a mere crack when the knocking came again, this time louder. Shock whitened her face at the first glimpse she caught of the man standing there. It wasn't the small boys, it was her husband, Brice Sinclair.

'Oh, no!' she gasped, too apprehensive to do more than stare. Her strength seemed to leave her, she couldn't even find enough to close the door in his face!

He looked terrible, ran her shocked thoughts. Strained, haggard, very pale. Aware that a runaway wife might be wiser to slam the door in the face of a pursuing husband, if she hoped to escape him, she was startled to hear herself murmuring, half-pityingly, 'Do you want to come in?'

'Yes,' he muttered hoarsely, without taking his eyes off her. 'If you'll let me?'

He wasn't exactly humble but he was different. Feeling numb, Macy stepped back as he entered and closed the door behind him. Then he turned to stare at her again.

From an intent scrutiny of her taut features, his eyes dropped slowly over her figure. A muscle in his throat worked as he appeared to be searching for his voice. 'You've had the baby?'

She nodded, having trouble with her own voice. 'Three weeks early.'

With a white ring of tension around his mouth, Brice asked savagely. 'How the hell did you manage?'

'Hospital,' she replied briefly, reluctant to remember how much she had missed him. The staff had been kind but she'd had no one of her own. 'I've been home three weeks.'

His glance left her a moment to swiftly encircle the room, his mouth twisting that she could call such a poor place home. 'Are you all right?'

'Yes.'

Distractedly, he ran a hand through his rumpled hair. He was as immaculately dressed as usual but Macy noticed how his eyes were bloodshot, as if he had been drinking too much or not sleeping well. He needed a shave too.

'The baby,' he visibly swallowed. 'A boy or girl?'

It was the baby he was concerned about. Macy winced, pointing to a crib in the corner. 'A boy—he's over there.'

Brice followed the direction of her hand. 'Can I see him?' and, as she nodded but frowned faintly, 'I promise not to wake him.' He stared towards the crib for a further moment, strangely hesitant, then in a few long strides he was over the room gazing down on his son.

Macy watched warily but felt curiously detached. She didn't seem to be feeling anymore. The numbness was still there and spreading. Brice might have been the doctor who occasionally looked in or someone she hadn't seen before.

He stood beside the crib his head bent, with red colour creeping into his averted cheek. He ran a hand over his eyes this time, but Macy couldn't believe he was brushing away a tear. Then slowly he lowered it, clenching and unclenching it until he was touching the baby's cheek with a tentative finger.

Macy thought he must have stood there for several minutes before returning to her, and all the time she was unable to move. She even felt beyond speech but as he approached within inches, she croaked the question that had only just occurred to her. 'How did you find me, Brice?'

Black eyes, not grey, fastened on her blankly. If she hadn't known better she might have thought he was in shock. 'It's not been easy. I looked ever since you went.'

'Because of the baby?'

'No!' he said roughly, clamping heavy hands on her shoulders. 'You! The baby might have been part of it.'

More likely the whole of it! Desperately she gazed at him. 'You can't take him away.'

His eyes slowly cleared of the awful blankness but remained fixed on her face. She wished they would return to their normal colour as well so she could guess what he was thinking. She wasn't prepared when he said grimly, 'I'm going to take you both away!'

'No!' she began shaking badly—she might have known he was up to something! 'This must be some trick . . .!'

'No trick.'

She interrupted sharply. 'Where are you planning to take us?'

'To live with me again.'

Her eyes flared wide open, the blue of the pupils dilating, becoming almost as dark as the ones staring down on her. The tension between them was suddenly terrible, a caged, wild thing, so dangerous neither dared breathe. When the baby whimpered, for Macy it was like a release. Wrenching from Brice's hold, she stumbled to see what was wrong but the baby didn't wake. Realising Brice was at her shoulder, she murmured absently, 'He's only dreaming.'

'Do they dream at that age?' he frowned.

Macy didn't answer. She was too busy thinking of what he had said. Clenching her hands tightly, she whispered, 'I can't live with you again, Brice. You don't trust me. Oh, I'm not blaming you,' she rushed on as he started to speak, 'how could you, under the circumstances, but I just can't stand it any more.'

'Macy!' he made her look at him, 'I do trust you, but I have to explain—we have to talk. Only, not here,' he said helplessly, for the first time that she could remember apparently at loss for words. 'If we talked here,' he managed at last, 'what I have to say mightn't sound right and we'd be back to square one. I know I've a nerve asking you to trust me when I didn't trust you before.'

'The circumstances aren't the same,' she said dully as he paused. Brice wasn't making sense and she shrank from exposing herself to further hurt.

'That's true,' he agreed, then, at her visible withdrawal, he burst out, 'For God's sake, Macy, have some pity on me.'

Had he ever had much for her? Fighting resentment, she looked away from him bleakly. 'I don't want to go back to Manchester, Brice. I'm not ready to face that yet. I'm sorry . . .'

'I'm not asking you to return there,' he exclaimed grimly, his voice steady again. 'I have a place here, in London. I've used it as a base while looking for you. I felt caged in a hotel, after the first few days.'

'A flat?'

'A house,' he said huskily, his eyes pleading. 'It's very nice. There's a garden where you could walk with the baby and a park just over the road.'

When she still hesitated, he asked hesitantly, 'What did you call him, by the way?'

'We never discussed it,' she replied stiffly, 'but I called him Richard, your second name, and for his second name, I gave him Mark, after my father.'

Brice looked pleased. 'Thank you.' His voice had an odd break in it. 'It sounds good, Richard Mark Sinclair. Better than I deserve.'

He talked of the baby but it was at Macy he gazed. His eyes fixed on her face as if he couldn't see enough of her. 'You haven't agreed to come with me,' he said, 'but don't you see, I can't leave you like this. If you won't move I'll have to stay with you here.'

Which would never work! Macy swallowed painfully. 'I'm trying to build a new life for myself and Richard.'

'Listen, Macy,' Brice begged, his tone taut but convincing. 'I'll make you a promise. Come for a month, during which time I'll not pressurise you in any way. No way at all,' he repeated, with such emphasis that she couldn't fail to understand what he meant. 'If at the end of the month you feel you can't live with me on any basis, I won't try and hold you. We have to talk, I've things to explain but, whatever the outcome, there'll be no pressure.'

Macy gazed at him helplessly for a few seconds then gave in. Everything inside her seemed dull, almost dead. She didn't think it was his pleading that swayed her so much as her own tiredness. If she had a month's respite to regain the strength she needed to become fully independent, it might also cure her of any lingering infatuation she had for her husband. She was halfway there, she realised, when she could look at him and feel nothing. And somehow she didn't doubt his word that he would let her go.

The move was swiftly accomplished for Macy had brought few personal belongings with her to London and accumulated very little since. Richard's crib was small, light enough to carry by hand and he had no pram. Brice's mouth tightened when she told him this but he merely retorted that it was no problem. They could shop for anything that was needed in the morning.

Hugging the baby tightly in her arms in the car, she hoped Brice didn't believe all their problems could be solved as easily. Looking at him sideways, she flushed as she met a glance as intent as her own and looked away again. He didn't seem like a man with everything under control, she had to admit. There was a greyness about him, a kind of bleakness she had never seen before. She couldn't believe his conscience was bothering him for, in a way, he'd been fair to her, so what was it? It would be natural for him to worry after she'd left for fear anything had happened to either her or the baby, but she couldn't believe he had been worried to the extent of making him look ten years older.

Her troubled thoughts were diverted as they arrived at a large house, at the end of a terrace overlooking Regent's Park. It was dark but the street lights clearly revealed a district very different from the one she had just left. After parking outside the front door, Brice came round to take the baby so that she could get out, and Macy saw the muscles of his throat jerk spasmodically as he held his son in his arms for the first time.

'I never thought it would happen in a London street,' she heard him mutter as he stared down on the baby's small sleeping face.

Something stirred in Macy then but it was gone in a flash before she could define what it was as, in firmer tones, Brice requested her to follow him and leave her things. He would come back for them later.

He would send a servant for them later didn't he mean? Macy braced herself to meet a veritable army of them lined up to meet their master's defaulting wife. To her surprise there was no one. The spacious hall was empty. The whole house echoed with a silence so profound that she turned to him with startled eyes. 'Where is everyone . . .?'

'I'm here alone,' he said gruffly.

'But the servants?' she tried to be more explicit, 'You usually have plenty.'

'I haven't got round to hiring any yet.' His red-rimmed eyes stared at her dully, 'I didn't think it was worth it. I haven't been in much. I've been too busy looking for you.'

If this had happened at Northholt, Macy would have been delighted. Recalling the fuss she had made, she realised the servants hadn't bothered her nearly as much as having nothing to do. If she had been involved in Brice's life, in the fullest sense of the word, she didn't think she would have resented either Mrs Bland or Miss Gregory. Here, she had Richard, if nothing else, to keep her busy. If there had been servants she might not have given them a second thought. Yet she was faintly relieved that there were no curious eyes to witness the final collapse of her marriage. Brice would let her go as soon as they reached an agreement over Richard. He would want access. She suspected this was the real reason why he had searched for her so diligently and brought her here. She prayed it wouldn't take longer than the four weeks he had stipulated.

He showed her the lounge and dining room, the kitchen and bedrooms upstairs. There were four bedrooms and a nursery, all tastefully decorated.

'Did you furnish the house yourself?' she asked wonderingly.

'No.' He stared at her uncomprehendingly for a moment. 'I took it over from a friend who's gone abroad for six months. I don't own it.'

Macy glanced at him in alarm. 'I'll have to be careful.'

'Don't worry.' He smiled grimly. 'He has kids of his own so you needn't be frightened of spilling anything.'

The baby began crying and a frown added to the lines on his brow. 'Is he ill, do you think? He could have caught a chill. It's a cold evening.'

'No,' Macy took him from Brice's arms, surprised to feel a twinge of jealousy. She didn't like how Richard's hand was curled round one of his father's fingers. He was almost difficult to prise away. Rather sharply, she said. 'He's only hungry.'

Brice didn't seem aware of her antagonism. He stared from his wife to his son anxiously. 'Have you his bottle?'

'Yes.' She hugged Richard against her shoulder. 'If we can go to the kitchen and you bring his things in, I can get it ready.'

In the kitchen, while she was busy, Brice stood watching, his face still pale. Hesitantly, he asked, 'You don't feed him yourself?'

Biting her lip, Macy shook her head, bending over Richard so Brice wouldn't see her expression. She had wanted to but she'd been ill and worried after he was born and unable to feed him herself. She'd been told that this wasn't uncommon in cases like hers but it hadn't decreased her sense of guilt.

After Richard was fed and changed, she let Brice carry him to the nursery again. He settled down without any fuss, although they waited until he had gone to sleep.

'He looks like you,' Macy admitted grudgingly.

'You don't approve?'

Startled by the tautness of Brice's voice, she shrugged non-committally. 'Sons often look like their fathers. Sometimes Richard acts like you too.'

'I hope not.'

Macy swallowed, unable to recognise the man she knew in this new Brice who displayed such bitter humility. Dazedly she looked at him and begged, 'Could I go to my room now, please?'

Brice met her eyes bleakly. 'Of course.'

He showed her into the one opposite the nursery over the corridor. He didn't insist she should share his and she was grateful. She didn't feel quite so relieved when he said. 'I'm next to you—there's a communicating door. I'd rather you were near for fear you need any help through the night.'

He meant with Richard. How did he think she had managed until now? Macy thanked him dully.

'You have your own bathroom.' He opened another door with the air of a man only vaguely conscious of what he was doing. 'If you want to freshen up, I'll go and make us something to eat.'

She hadn't known he could cook. Her eyes widening in surprise, she said hastily. 'Nothing for me, thanks, but I would love a bath. I haven't had a proper one since leaving hospital.' When he frowned she explained. 'There was a bathroom where I lived but with ten other people sharing there was never any hot water.'

Anger leapt from Brice's eyes until he visibly controlled it. 'All right,' he said grimly. 'Have a good soak and I'll bring you some hot milk later.'

As soon as he had gone, she took her night things from the case he'd brought up earlier and carried them through to the bathroom. The house was lovely and warm. She hadn't realised how cold she had been, relying on a small electric fire not big enough to heat a room properly. The bath revived her, she had almost forgotten what it was to indulge in such a luxury. It seemed a long time since she had felt so clean. When she stepped out reluctantly, the lethargy was still there but physically she felt better.

Pulling on her nightdress and négligé, it no longer mattered that they were so thin, although she felt strangely self-conscious about Brice seeing her in them. After brushing her hair and smoothing a little moisture cream into her face, she wondered if she'd have time to slip into bed before he returned.

She wasn't prepared to find him sitting on the edge of her bed, his eyes riveted on the bathroom door. Overwhelmed by confusion, Macy nearly turned and ran but something in the depth of his eyes held her. It was that hint of unfamiliar pleading which had brought her against her will to his house this evening, and which she still found difficult to resist. It was as new to her as it was, she suspected, to him, and it influenced her, in her present state of weakness, more than arrogance might have done.

'Don't go away,' he muttered hoarsely, jumping to his feet. He gestured towards a flask and cup with biscuits set on a tray by the bedside. 'I brought your milk and we have to talk.'

'Richard . . .' she had never thought of him as a means of escape before. She did now but Brice forestalled her. 'I've just checked, he's sleeping soundly. And I've set the alarm system connecting with my room.'

About to pass him, Macy paused. He still thought of everything. Helplessly she gazed at him, not for the first time resenting such sheer efficiency. 'If you're sure?' she said uncertainly.

'I think I can manage my own son,' he retorted heavily, 'I'll even have a go at changing him, but it's you I'm worried about. I want to talk to you, Macy, there's a lot to explain, but I can't if you won't listen.'

He stepped nearer as if desperately trying to find some means of convincing her he was in earnest. His eyes darkened as they roved over her slender body, lingering where the skin of her neck and shoulders was as smooth as silk. She saw him swallow as if his throat was hurting and a pulse jerked at the side of his mouth. She felt his glance burning through the scanty covering of her négligé before he tore his eyes away.

'I realise you're tired and still far from well,' he said thickly, 'but I think you'd sleep better if you heard what I have to say.'

Macy found it difficult to believe he could tell her anything she didn't already know. How could he alter basic facts? She had done wrong and Brice had married her impulsively for the sake of the firm. They both had regrets and even if he told her he had decided to trust her it would be an empty gesture. Besides, she wouldn't be satisfied with only his trust now. Greed had no limits, she mocked with self-scorn. She also wanted his love!

'I'll listen—if you really think there's any point,' she agreed bleakly. 'But trust can't be the result of a sudden decision, Brice. It has to grow.'

'Macy,' he groaned, aware of her white cheeks and

shaking limbs. 'Come on, get into bed. You'll find it easier to listen there.'

A moment later she was under the sheets while he sat beside her, holding her hand tightly, refusing to let it go. He was thinner, she realised, tensing as some feeling shot through her but unable to take her eyes off his haggard face. The bed was comfortable but suddenly she could only think of him. His haunted eyes troubled her, she felt pity although she tried to fight it. 'What is it?' she whispered.

'First,' he said, his mouth twisting, 'let's go back to when we first met. We were obviously attracted to each other. You were—and still are—a beautiful, charming girl, and I wanted an affair with you. I had, in fact, decided on it, and with women,' he shrugged wryly, 'I was used to getting my own way. Then, when things weren't going quite as easily as I had anticipated, I received that anonymous letter about your designs and everything blew up in my face.'

'You don't have to go into all that again,' Macy pleaded unhappily, feeling unable to bear it. 'I know all about it.'

'But not my side of the story,' he reminded her thinly. 'Please. Macy...'

'Go on then,' she said churlishly.

To her surprise he didn't take exception to her discouraging tones. It was as if he considered he deserved nothing better.

'If I hadn't been so—emotionally involved with you,' he continued carefully, 'I might have stopped to take a look at the whole thing properly. The letter accused you of breaking your agreement with the firm for personal gain. When I asked Miss Drake, without revealing any details, of course, what the agreement consisted of, she quoted from one in the files that it forbade employees to design for, or to sell a design to, another firm while working for us. What she didn't say—and what I didn't discover until I returned from the States—was that that agreement. based on a considerable rise in salary, only applied to employees who had been with us five years. Which absolved you completely.'

Macy drew a sharp breath. She felt completely bewildered to say the least. 'But—I signed an agreement . . .!'

'Just one concerning a starting wage and the usual regulations concerning general conditions such as holidays.'

'But, Thelma said . . .'

'It's fairly clear what Thelma said,' Brice cut in harshly. 'She was after your allegiance from the beginning and you obviously didn't study your contract closely.'

'She said it wasn't necessary,' Macy remembered. 'She said it just said things like what you quoted and that I hadn't to work for another firm. When she persuaded me to do that design for her brother, she warned me, if I was found out, the penalties could be severe.'

'She wanted to frighten you,' Brice retorted tightly. 'In fact, it's been discovered since then that she's been selling designs herself, all along. She involved you because she was suddenly frightened of being found out and wanted a scapegoat. Actually it was her design that won the competition for her brother but in giving you some of the prize money she obviously considered it a cheap way of providing herself with an alibi, should anything go wrong.'

Macy stared at him. She knew she should be feeling a sense of relief at what Brice was saying, but somehow it was so incredible she couldn't take it in. 'How do you know it was Thelma's design that won the competition?'

Recognising she needed convincing, Brice was more explicit. 'I had someone on to it as soon as I got suspicious. Miss Brown's work is unmistakable, very bold, very impressive, with a definite appeal for foreign buyers. Comparing it with yours isn't possible. It's like comparing exotic jungle blooms with an Alpine meadow.'

'But why did she go away, do you think?' Macy frowned.

Brice's eyes darkened with anger. 'The pace was getting too hot for her. When I realised she must have written that letter condemning you, I had a feeling then, though no proof, that she was somehow responsible for the whole sorry business. Maybe my suspicions showed more than I realised, for after I talked to her she clearly took fright. This is why, I believe, she's been keeping in touch with her old colleagues in the department. It's rather like a murderer returning to the scene of the crime. She's been trying to find out if any of her questionable activities have come to light.'

Some relief stirred in Macy at last, a lessening of the guilt that had haunted her for so long, but there were still so many questions. 'You were very angry with me,' she said slowly.

'I was,' Brice's face grew paler as he met her anguished eyes. 'I think it was a culmination of many things—frustration, resentment that you had fallen off the pedestal I had you on. It was as if an angel I worshipped had crashed at my feet and I went more than a little crazy.'

'You didn't have to marry me,' she whispered.

'No, I didn't.' A muscle jerked in his cheek. 'But, like I said at the time, Macy, I had to have you. You were in my blood, you'd become an obsession, and I realised it would be almost impossible, after what had happened, to continue our relationship as I'd intended. Marriage seemed the only way and I admit I exaggerated your so-called crime as much as I could to frighten you so much you wouldn't dare do anything but what I asked. I had the advantage of your family problems too, which I knew weighed heavily in my favour.'

Macy stared at his gaunt face, his eyes dark with

suffering, yet she felt no pity. 'So now you feel you can trust me again,' she said bitterly.

'I did before I discovered all this,' Brice confessed tautly. 'Remember the evening we went to the Alstons' party and I was dancing with their daughter?' When Macy nodded reluctantly, he went on, 'She began hinting outrageously about you having conned the firm and though I sensed she was half-guessing it made me see red. I knew then that you weren't capable of deceit of any kind, that if you had done something wrong it had been for Kate's sake and nothing else. I realised then that I trusted you completely.'

Could she believe him? Doubt trembled through Macy as she wondered suspiciously why he hadn't told her this before? And as if he had read her thoughts, he hesitated and explained huskily. 'I had to go to the States, Macy. I had to have time to clear my mind. I didn't think it was any good just saying that I trusted you when you were so weighed down with your own sense of guilt. I kept thinking of what you had said about Thelma writing letters and somehow I knew instinctively that while there might be some investigating to be done, I could clear you completely. Not for my sake but yours,' he added grimly, as she still frowned doubtfully. 'I already had a good idea where to begin, only when I arrived home you had gone.'

'I couldn't stay, Brice,' she whispered. 'I couldn't bear having you always treating me so suspiciously.'

'I realise now, Macy,' he swallowed painfully. 'I made life hell for you but you would forgive me if you knew how I felt when I found you'd disappeared.'

'Yet you still went ahead with your investigations?'

He nodded. 'With the aid of expert assistance—as I was looking for you, but the whole story wasn't pieced together until a few days ago.'

Macy asked apprehensively. 'Will you do anything about Thelma?' Thelma had hurt her but she had no desire for revenge.

'No, she's gone now.' He paused, his eyes darkening anxiously. 'As far as I'm concerned, it's all over. I hope you can feel the same way, Macy?'

'I'll try,' she murmured, wondering if it would be possible, not sure what was in her heart.

'As far as trust goes, you have mine forever,' Brice squeezed her hand.

His fingers on hers were conveying something but she felt nothing. 'Thank you,' she whispered, confused that something she had hungered for so desperately should leave her feeling so empty.

Brice stared at her in anguish, his eyes wandering to her mouth but averting quickly. As though he feared his control was slipping, he jumped to his feet. 'I'm hoping this is going to make a difference to how you feel about staying with me, Macy. I promised not to pressurise you but I think we should stay together, if only for the sake of the baby.'

For the baby's sake! Over the next few weeks Macy couldn't get the words out of her head. If only Brice had said for her sake, or that he had loved her. There was no doubting his love for Richard, which betrayed itself in so many ways, but he had none for her. Sometimes she thought her heart would break for as the numbness that had prevailed during the first week of living with Brice wore off she felt unable to bear the pain.

Brice worked mostly in the small study next to the breakfast room. He had offices in the city but he preferred to bring his work home with him. The greater part of each day though, he devoted to his family. He was proving to be such a wonderful father that Macy didn't know how she was going to part him from his son. She sensed he would like to be closer to her as well and his drawn face revealed he was worrying over the decision she must finally make as to whether she would stay with him or not. But she still couldn't be sure of his trust, nor did she feel she could live with him again when he didn't love her. Sometimes, in the night, when her treacherous body hungered for him, it took every bit of willpower she had to remain in her own bed and not go to him.

One evening, just when she had finished giving Richard his ten o'clock feed, Brice came to the nursery with a letter for her. It had come with a bundle from Manchester, he said, but he hadn't discovered they weren't all for him until a few minutes ago.

'Oh!' Macy put Richard in his cot so she could open it. It was from Miss Kirby. 'How nice,' she smiled, telling Brice whom it was from. 'She's in between jobs,' she murmured, reading bits aloud. 'She's been nursing another . . .' Macy swallowed, 'patient who has died. Now she thinks she would like to try children for a change.'

Brice smiled. 'Would that be a hint, do you think? Would she like to come to us?'

'Us?' Macy stared at him trying to hide the way she flinched. Was he looking for someone to take care of Richard after she had gone? She had been thinking of taking Richard from him but it seemed it could be the other way round!

Then he confused her again by saying. 'If you stay with me, Macy, I should want you by my side as a real wife, which would mean social functions and entertaining occasionally, as well as trips overseas. We couldn't take Richard everywhere.'

And Miss Kirby would be ideal—as yet just in her fifties and someone they both trusted. Quickly, Macy shrugged the thought—the temptation—aside while she could still resist it. 'I'm afraid I won't be staying with you,' she replied, her voice cracking a little but remarkably convincing. 'I just don't think it would work out!' she cried as he went white. 'It was only sex between us, wasn't it? You would only make me unhappy.'

She wasn't prepared for how he turned abruptly and

left her without another word—no indication of his reactions apart from a glimpse of something dying in his eyes. She heard his footsteps going downstairs like those of an old man.

Richard was sleeping. Macy stared down at him, gripping the rail of his cot with hands on which the knuckles showed white. What had she done! Outside, the February night was stormy with sleet and snow battering on the window but she didn't hear it. Her thoughts were too concentrated on her own stupidity. She had sent Brice away, perhaps for good, for she'd been too full of self-pity to see anything from his point of view. Now, as a different aspect of the situation struck her, shock ricocheted through her.

When she had done the design for Thelma's brother, she had believed she was breaking the rules, so technically, at least, she'd been in the wrong. Yet Brice, knowing this, had learned to trust her. What was wrong with their marriage now was that she didn't trust him. She had wanted his love yet hadn't he shown it to her in so many ways? She had thought it was his conscience prodding him but wouldn't it take more than that to produce the devotion he had shown so unfailingly since he had brought her here? Suddenly Macy felt small and ashamed. In return for all the help and consideration he'd given her she'd distrusted his motives to a far greater extent than he had ever distrusted hers.

Suddenly she let go of the cot, hurrying to her room, where she showered and put on a fresh négligé before going downstairs. With uneven breath, she knocked lightly on the study door but without waiting for an answer walked straight in. Brice was sitting at his desk, head in hands, studying some papers but as soon as he heard her he looked up, asking quickly, with a hint of alarm in the dullness of his eyes, if there was something wrong?

'There has been,' Macy's voice croaked but she forced herself to go on. 'Something I have to put right.'

Again she swallowed, 'I've come to tell you that I love you, Brice, and if you want me to stay I will. I realise you don't love me but perhaps . . .'

She had been about to say—perhaps in time, but before she could get it out, with a strangled curse for the chair that got in his way, Brice was at his side, pulling her into his arms. His eyes glittering, he gasped hoarsely. 'Will you say that again, Macy?'

'I'll stay.'

'No—Yes, that too.' Gaining momentum his voice rolled like thunder. 'But the other!'

'I love you!' she whispered, beginning to cry softly.

'Oh, God! Macy.' The tears suddenly fell from him in front of her tear-blurred eyes, 'I never thought to hear you say that. Please don't cry.'

The way his haggard face cleared stunned her to silence, reward in itself. It was worth any sacrifice of pride to see at least some of the pain fading. 'You care for me?' she asked wonderingly, at the unashamed moisture in his eyes.

'Care for you!' With a kind of ruthless impatience he couldn't find any other way to express, his arms tightened and he covered her mouth with his own. 'Care for you,' he muttered thickly against her lips, 'I love you, worship you, woman!'

A hot flame shot through Macy as soon as his mouth found hers, making her head swim and her legs go weak. She might have fallen if he hadn't been holding her as uncontrollable passion flared between them, rapidly bounding out of control.

'It's been so long,' he groaned, lifting her off the floor as if she was no weight at all and striding with her from the study upstairs to his bedroom. He was like a man possessed and Macy in a similar state of abandonment as he laid her on the bed and disposed of their clothing in what seemed like one fluid movement. The coming together of their bodies aroused her to a frenzy she was beyond trying to hide.

CAPTIVE OF FATE 185

'I want you,' she moaned as he came down beside her and she shuddered violently, her blue eyes filling with tears.

'Do you think I don't know, my darling,' he muttered. 'You aren't the only one who can't wait.'

When he pulled her head back and kissed her open mouth, the desire between them which had lain dormant for weeks suddenly surged outside anything they had previously experienced. What Macy had been going to say faded with her thoughts into a kind of enchanted delirium. Feeling his hands cupping her breasts, his thumbs teasing her sensitive nipples, she could only cling to him, her nails digging into his broad shoulders in an effort to convey the overwhelming state of her needs.

Brice's mouth was devouring hungrily. It roamed all over her, threatening to drive her to the brink of insanity, none of his caresses anything but a prelude to a fiercely driving necessity to possess her. He showed no mercy but she didn't want any. He held her so powerfully and she craved him so much that she welcomed the final invasion of his body with a blind disregard for any pain. As her slender limbs melted into his, she thought she must be dying of a rapture she had never hoped to experience again. She wasn't even conscious of crying his name as they sped upwards together in an explosion of passion so devastating that she never expected to come down to earth again.

It was minutes after that soul-shaking culmination before she stopped trembling and Brice shuddering. At last he raised himself on an elbow to stare down on her flushed face, her dazed, radiant eyes and long silky hair spread out on the pillow. His own face was hot, with a dampness to his skin Macy could feel as she raised a suddenly shy hand to touch his cheek. 'I find it difficult to believe that anything could be better between us than it was before, but that was perfect,' he said huskily.

'Because we discovered we love each other?' Macy whispered, adoring him with her eyes.

'You don't know what these past weeks have been like,' he uttered, a brief darkening to his pupils. 'Having you so near and unable to touch you.'

'I realised how wrong I'd been,' Macy confessed, 'but I didn't guess you loved me.'

'I discovered I loved you when I was in the States,' he said slowly, 'but I think I loved you from the very beginning. I know I could never contemplate losing you, not even when I thought I hated you. That's why I kept you so short of money—anything to lessen the risk of you running away. And I felt like murdering Tim Matthews or any man who looked at you.'

'I sold my car to help me get to London,' Macy owned uncertainly.

He nodded. 'I thought you'd taken it with you until the gardener told me. Oh, God!' he groaned, burying his face in her hair, so she couldn't see his remembered torment. 'I thought I was going berserk trying to find you until one hotel remembered a certain very pregnant lady.'

'I missed you when Richard was born,' she whispered, 'I really suffered for leaving you then.'

'Not half as much as I suffered being away from you,' he said starkly.

'Brice,' she hesitated, 'I want to be a good wife to you but I'm still not sure about returning to Manchester.'

He dropped passionate little kisses on her face. 'We'll start again, my sweet. I'll ring Miss Kirby in the morning and as soon as she gets here we'll all fly to L.A. You'll love it there, darling.' His voice was suddenly very eager. 'Once Richard settles down I intend taking you for a honeymoon. Even a week or two together is my idea of heaven.'

'Mine, too,' she breathed, looking into his glowing eyes, 'I love you, Brice, darling.'

He made an inarticulate sound as his mouth moved against her throat, then said, very softly, 'I love you too, Mrs Sinclair.'

His hand caressed her breast gently but she could feel desire stirring in him again. With a sensuous sigh of pleasure, she curled softly against him, like a kitten. It seemed a miracle had happened tonight. Some people didn't believe in them but she wasn't going to question it. She was going to spend the rest of her life being part of it, wasn't she? Tightly her arms went around her husband and with a groan of satisfaction he pressed her closer while his hand went out to put out the light.

ROMANCE

Variety is the spice of romance

Each month, Mills & Boon publish new romances. New stories about people falling in love. A world of variety in romance — from the best writers in the romantic world. Choose from these titles in April.

TEMPORARY HUSBAND Susan Alexander
LADY WITH A PAST Lillian Cheatham
PASSION'S VINE Elizabeth Graham
THE SIX-MONTH MARRIAGE Penny Jordan
ICE PRINCESS Madeleine Ker
ACT OF POSSESSION Anne Mather
A NO RISK AFFAIR Carole Mortimer
CAPTIVE OF FATE Margaret Pargeter
ALIEN VENGEANCE Sara Craven
THE WINGS OF LOVE Sally Wentworth

On sale where you buy paperbacks. If you require further information or have any difficulty obtaining them, write to: Mills & Boon Reader Service, PO Box 236, Thornton Road, Croydon, Surrey CR9 3RU, England.

Mills & Boon
the rose of romance

ROMANCE

Next month's romances from Mills & Boon

Each month, you can choose from a world of variety in romance with Mills & Boon. These are the new titles to look out for next month.

CAPRICORN MAN Jacqueline Gilbert
BUSHRANGER'S MOUNTAIN Victoria Gordon
BIG SUR Elizabeth Graham
THE OBJECT OF THE GAME Vanessa James
TAKEN OVER Penny Jordan
HOSTAGE Madeleine Ker
DARK OBSESSION Valerie Marsh
TRUST IN TOMORROW Carole Mortimer
MODEL OF DECEPTION Margaret Pargeter
DOUBLE DECEPTION Kay Thorpe

Buy them from your usual paperback stockist, or write to: Mills & Boon Reader Service, P.O. Box 236, Thornton Rd, Croydon, Surrey CR9 3RU, England. Readers in South Africa write to: Mills & Boon Reader Service of Southern Africa, Private Bag X3010, Randburg, 2125.

Mills & Boon
the rose of romance

Best Seller Romances

These best loved romances are back

Mills & Boon Best Seller Romances are the love stories that have proved particularly popular with our readers. These are the titles to look out for this month.

STRANGE BEDFELLOW
Janet Dailey
TEMPTATION
Charlotte Lamb
THE RIVER ROOM
Anne Weale

Buy them from your usual paperback stockist, or write to: Mills & Boon Reader Service, P.O. Box 236, Thornton Rd, Croydon, Surrey CR9 3RU, England. Readers in South Africa-write to: Mills & Boon Reader Service of Southern Africa, Private Bag X3010, Randburg, 2125.

Mills & Boon
the rose of romance

Mills & Boon

Take 4 Exciting Books Absolutely FREE

Love, romance, intrigue... all are captured for you by Mills & Boon's top-selling authors. By becoming a regular reader of Mills & Boon's Romances you can enjoy 6 superb new titles every month plus a whole range of special benefits: your very own personal membership card, a free monthly newsletter packed with recipes, competitions, exclusive book offers and a monthly guide to the stars, plus extra bargain offers and big cash savings.

**AND an Introductory FREE GIFT for YOU.
Turn over the page for details.**

As a special introduction we will send you four exciting Mills & Boon Romances Free and without obligation when you complete and return this coupon.

At the same time we will reserve a subscription to Mills & Boon Reader Service for you. Every month, you will receive 6 of the very latest novels by leading Romantic Fiction authors, delivered direct to your door. You don't pay extra for delivery — postage and packing is always completely Free. There is no obligation or commitment — you can cancel your subscription at any time.

You have nothing to lose and a whole world of romance to gain.

Just fill in and post the coupon today to MILLS & BOON READER SERVICE, FREEPOST, P.O. BOX 236, CROYDON, SURREY CR9 9EL.

Please Note:- READERS IN SOUTH AFRICA write to
**Mills & Boon, Postbag X3010,
Randburg 2125, S. Africa.**

FREE BOOKS CERTIFICATE

To: Mills & Boon Reader Service, FREEPOST, P.O. Box 236, Croydon, Surrey CR9 9EL.

Please send me, free and without obligation, four Mills & Boon Romances, and reserve a Reader Service Subscription for me. If I decide to subscribe I shall, from the beginning of the month following my free parcel of books, receive six new books each month for £6.60, post and packing free. If I decide not to subscribe, I shall write to you within 10 days. The free books are mine to keep in any case. I understand that I may cancel my subscription at any time simply by writing to you. I am over 18 years of age.

Please write in BLOCK CAPITALS.

Signature _____

Name _____

Address _____

_____ Post code _____

SEND NO MONEY — TAKE NO RISKS.
Please don't forget to include your Postcode.
Remember, postcodes speed delivery. Offer applies in UK only and is not valid to present subscribers. Mills & Boon reserve the right to exercise discretion in granting membership. If price changes are necessary you will be notified.
Offer expires 31st December 1985